THE SHADOW OF A SHADOW

R. H. DIXON

CORVUS CORONE PRESS

Front cover by Carrion Crow Design.

A CIP catalogue record for this title is available from the British Library.

ISBN: 978-1-9997180-8-4

Corvus Corone Press.

For Marvin; the greatest, cleverest, funniest, most loving little boy we could ever have hoped for. You captured our hearts on the very first day and left them utterly broken on your last.

Other books by R. H. Dixon:

**EMERGENCE
A STORYTELLING OF RAVENS
CRIBBINS**

THE SULLIVAN CARTER SERIES:
THE CUNDY (BOOK #1)

'I want you to believe... to believe in things that you cannot.'
Bram Stoker, *Dracula*

1

Maureen Hall

1978

Rain beat against the windows and wind howled around the sturdy hundred-year-old structure of Eden House, baying to be let inside, to run mad in its corridors. Above the noise, Maureen Hall could hear her sister, Jeanette, whimpering in the next bed; a soft, muffled sound, barely there but more than enough to secure an unbridled thrashing if Sister Gregory was to pass their dormitory. All the kids at Eden House, perhaps the old folk too, had received beatings for much less 'disruptive behaviour'. Last month, Sister Gregory had caned the bottom of Maureen's feet so hard with Mr Birchwood – a cane she always carried, and her preferred tool of torture – she hadn't been able to walk for three days, all because she'd sneezed during Sunday service.

Jeanette was on a behavioural warning already. She'd sparked the wrath of the old nun only that morning for having wet the bed. Bed-wetting's for babies and sissies. No wonder your parents died, so they could get away from you, Sister Gregory had said, before ordering Jeanette to strip to her underwear. You're a nuisance. A noose around society's neck. She'd then beat the back of Jeanette's legs with Mr Birchwood till welts oozed there. Afterwards, Jeanette was made to stand at the foot of her bed in her damp knickers while all the other kids went for breakfast.

Sister Gregory demanded she balanced the urine-soaked bedsheet on top of her head too, as an extra punishment for being a 'dirty little pig'. She'd stood like that for almost an hour.

Maureen couldn't remember a time when Jeanette hadn't been a nervous child, but this disposition of hers got worse the longer they stayed at Eden House. The bed-wetting was becoming more and more frequent. They'd been there just over a year now, following the death of their parents in a motorway collision. With no other family, at least none that was able (or willing) to take them in, their upbringing and welfare had fallen to the government's care system. Only, the government's care system had failed them entirely by entrusting them to the Sisters of Eden.

A care centre for orphans, delinquent youths – whom no one knew what else to do with – and the infirm elderly, Eden House was a mixed-bag-residence for some of Yorkshire's most unfortunate and/or troublesome ones. Brooding in its own five acres of land, it was an imposing old building in the suburbs of Sheffield. It had a black double door to the front, positioned centrally like a comedy moustache which no one found funny. The upper layer of the building had Dormer windows and was topped with slate tiles. On a dry day Eden House had a greying pate, but on a wet day it had a slick black crown.

An inbuilt chapel, complete with a bell tower, formed the entire east wing. It contained nothing more exciting than creaking wooden benches, an ancient-looking organ, hymn books from another era and the smell of dust. Hymn singing was mandatory (and you'd better sing like you meant it!) and all prayers were said in vain. No matter its occupancy, the chapel was an empty-sounding space which reverberated all noises; a hollowness you could feel in your innards. Maureen imagined the walls emitted a dry, papery laugh during the restlessness of night when no one was around; one you might hear from any of the dormitories if you listened hard enough. Maureen tried not to.

During daylight hours, Eden House's burnt-orange bricks gave an austere air of oppressive authority, and rows of white-framed windows on all three floors hinted at the uniform way in which the Sisters of Eden conducted business on the inside. At night time, Eden House looked nightmarish. A hulking, black-silhouetted terror that threatened to snatch non-residents if they strayed too close. A watchful monster, ready to strike. Tonight, it sounded like a nightmare too – on the inside, at least. The wind and rain battered the nuns' fortress like a legion of demons, all of them howling and scratching. Let us in. Let us in.

Above the racket of the squall, Jeanette's sobbing persisted. Maureen willed her to be quiet. Knew it was only a matter of time before Sister Gregory would detect the disturbance. Nothing got past the old despot. In fact, Maureen reckoned she was already sniffing out those who weren't asleep. Like a witch or troll from the worst kind of fairy tale, her Roman nose would be upturned, nostrils quivering, and the hair follicles all over her body would act like receptors to Jeanette's anguish. She pictured Mr Birchwood clutched in her gnarled, rough hands, already twitching. Maureen felt sick with dread.

Night time at Eden House presented a different set of dangers to those during the day. It was never a safe place. During the day, Sister Gregory stomped about in wooden clogs. She loved being loud, thrived on the fear her presence invoked. But by night she prowled barefooted, so she had the element of surprise. Had a propensity for night time sneaking. Was always creeping. If Sister Gregory slept, none of the kids knew when or where. Badness fuelled her, of which she seemed to have an endless supply. Perhaps Eden House itself energised her.

When the lights went out, she was worse than most of the imagined monsters in cupboards or ghouls under the bed. The fear Mr Birchwood might rap an exposed ankle or wrist saw that Eden House's residents kept themselves covered from chin to toe with their bedclothes throughout the night.

When she was younger, Maureen had assumed all nuns were righteous. A little stuffy, perhaps, and strange-looking in their habits, but all of them caring and compassionate. Now, however, she knew better. Sister Gregory was the worst of them all, but if there was a single nun within Eden House who had an ounce of empathy, Maureen had yet to meet her. She had no option but to think they were all bitter and twisted psychopaths who hid their evilness behind the black shrouds of assumed godliness they wore. The nuns of Eden House lacked any sense of love and compassion and, instead, enjoyed the sport of inflicting physical pain and mental suffering upon those in their care. Maureen had decided months ago that if God condoned their actions, which she had no choice but to think He did because He sure as hell had answered none of her prayers, then she wanted nothing more to do with Him.

The dormitory she and Jeanette slept in had twelve beds in total; each with a metal frame, starched white sheet and scratchy grey wool blanket. The only adornment on the plain, skimmed walls was a clock and a wooden cross holding a figurine of Jesus, to remind them of their unending misery. During the day Jesus looked like a pained wraith trying to escape his fiery teak-red bonds. At night, the blackness of those bonds absorbed him. The cross was like a hole burnt into the plaster from which snakes slithered. Maureen saw them often. She heard them every night in the walls.

She and Jeanette shared this draughty, prison-like room with ten other girls whose ages ranged from three to sixteen. It was Joanna Blakelock, a chubby-cheeked three-year-old, for whom Maureen felt especially sorry. Poor Joanna had many more years of Eden House to endure; the kind of timeframe that could break a mind. Perhaps a body too. Maureen was thankful she had Jeanette and happy memories of a stable, loving family life before Eden House. But Joanna Blakelock had no one else in the world and was likely too young to maintain clear recollections of a life before the tyranny of the nuns. The older girls tried to mother Joanna sometimes, but at the risk of being beaten for 'mollycoddling' all too often they neglected to get involved.

Parquet floors and high-ceilinged rooms throughout the entire building collected and held many dark secrets. Eden House was a disturbed place, haunted by most of those ever associated with it, dead or alive. Maureen knew of these ghosts all too well. She spent hours contemplating whether they and the nuns would let her live till the time she could leave Eden House.

Seven years to go.

It seemed like a lifetime. But it could be worse, she knew. Much, much worse. She could be Joanna Blakelock.

From her bed, Maureen watched the deep shadows that decked the room, especially the area of insidious darkness near the open door, in case anything moved. Nothing did. She couldn't detect any creeping sounds either. No slap of bare feet, soft or otherwise, on parquet. No billowing of black cloth. There was only the soft but insistent sound of Jeanette whimpering, the wind slicing across the face of the building, screaming through gaps in masonry, and the harsh demon-nail *tick-tick* of rain on the windows. Taking a deep breath, Maureen slid out of bed and darted towards Jeanette's. The hard floor was cold against the soles of her feet and the darkness smothered her in a prickly embrace, making her shudder and worry she'd misjudged the shadows. Because what if they contained something even worse than the nuns?

He'll eat your heart, eat your eyes…

Stop it.

Maureen slipped beneath Jeanette's covers, immediately sensing her sister's body stiffen. She searched for her hand and found it. Jeanette accepted Maureen's interlocking fingers between hers, then relaxed and huddled close. They lay together, unspeaking. Comforted by each other's warmth and the rhythmic synchronicity of their breathing. Maureen had only intended to stay for a few minutes, but their embrace must have been too soothing because soon she fell asleep. She dreamt that she and Jeanette were back at home with their parents, all of them playing Monopoly at the dining table. She only had five pounds in the bank, but it didn't matter because they were all laughing and talking. All of them together.

It was still dark when Maureen awoke. At first she wasn't aware that anything was wrong, but as the allure of her dream faded and she became mindful of Jeanette's arm resting on her own, the shock of reality hit her and she remembered she was in the wrong bed.

Her heart quickened.

Oh no oh no oh no.

How could she have been so careless?

The rain had eased, but the gale still battered the front of the building. It pressed its featureless face against the window, almost hard enough to make it implode. Maureen lifted Jeanette's arm in readiness to flee to the safety of her own bed, but froze when she saw a dark shape looming. A tall, black-veiled apparition moving closer and closer. Snakes began to pour from the cross-shaped hole in the wall, hissing as their bodies knotted and unknotted. Maureen pushed herself against the mattress, hoping to become invisible.

Don't see me, I'm not here.

There was a swift whooshing sound and a sharp crack of pain shot across her shin bones. She gritted her teeth, stifling a cry. Next to her, Jeanette jolted upright with a yelp.

'What outrageous devilment is this?' It was Sister Gregory. Her voice a low, throaty growl awful enough to scare the snakes, which fell silent, some of them re-joining Jesus in the wall.

Neither Maureen nor Jeanette responded. There was no right answer. Beyond all confinement, wind screamed. Sister Gregory threw back the bedcovers and gripped Maureen by the arm, hoisting her upwards. This time Maureen cried out. The night air penetrated the thin cotton of her nightdress, coating her body with a hostile chill, thus making her limbs become rigid. The old nun's fingernails were like talons biting into her flesh. Sharp enough, Maureen thought, to puncture muscle, sever nerves and scrape bone. She imagined Sister Gregory was a black-feathered siren of Satan; a not-so-mythological bird-like beast that had swooped down to snatch her and Jeanette up and carry them off to some room of torture. She scrunched her eyes and ground her teeth as she was forced to her feet.

The other girls in the dormitory pretended not to watch, but were too quiet and still to be sleeping. Nests of snakes writhed on their beds.

Next, Sister Gregory dragged Jeanette across the mattress. Jeanette clutched at the dry bedsheets as if they might save her from whatever beating she'd get – Look, Sister Gregory, I didn't wet the bed. But the old nun didn't care, there'd be no leniency. Never was. She pulled Jeanette to her feet next to Maureen, then stooped low, her face a paradigm of witchy hag; sharp elongated features, grey-ish skin drained of youth, sunken eyes, could be hollow sockets, and an upper lip crested by sparse, bristly hair, much like nylon poking through a threadbare rag. She opened her mouth and Maureen watched a long stringy insect escape from the black hole. It scurried across her sunken, waxy cheek, then disappeared into the blackness of her veil.

'Night time larking will not be tolerated.' Her breath was like a flash of rancid, fishy meat. 'Come with me, you insolent little pigs.' She turned and marched towards the door, her feet smacking against the wooden floor because she was no longer creeping. Was pleased to affirm her presence to anyone else who dared to be awake. When she reached the door, she said, 'Everyone else, back to sleep NOW. Or there'll be five lashes for every single one of you in the morning.'

Jeanette grabbed for Maureen's hand and held it tight. Maureen squeezed back; a reflexive gesture of basic reassurance that felt empty. An urge to flee, to take Jeanette with her through the corridors and down the stairs and out through the front door overcame Maureen. But they had nowhere else to go. Nowhere to hide. They'd be found and returned, then there'd be even bigger repercussions. Who knew, Satan's siren might carry them all the way to Hell. So they had no alternative but to follow Sister Gregory wherever she might think to take them.

They traipsed along dark, echoing corridors, none of which were lit. Gusts of wind blasted the front end of the care home, creating angry shrieks at the north-facing windows. The fabric of Sister Gregory's black robe shushed as she walked. An angry ruffling sound. Might well be feathers, Maureen thought. They passed the doors of dormitories where other girls and boys slept, but soon Maureen lost all sense of where they were and wondered if there were parts of Eden House's upper floor she hadn't known existed. None of it seemed right. Passageways were too long. Too meandering. Too labyrinthine. The whole building creaked and strained under the persistence of the storm. Maureen hoped the entire roof would blow off. That the wind would sweep Sister Gregory away and impale her on one of the metal spikes at the entrance gates. But the roof remained intact. Continued to box them in this unreliable maze of innumerable rooms and their infamous stories. Stories which held no logical weight, yet were told and retold and believed as standard.

They crept past a painting of the Virgin Mary. Greyness shrouded her in brushstroke swathes of rigid-looking material, and she grinned in a way that wasn't in the least bit holy. Her dark eyes, unblinking, followed Maureen and Jeanette. Maureen watched as an earthworm wriggled free from the glistening corner of her right eye. It fell to the floor with a soft splat, then squirmed there. Muted flies swarmed the blank areas of the canvas, rising from the virgin's headdress. Maureen gripped Jeanette's hand tighter and quickened her pace.

Eventually, Sister Gregory came to a stop outside a door. It might lead anywhere, Maureen thought. Eden House's interior doors were all the same: stained oak with round metal handles, each with a lock, not always a key. This one had a key.

'If you want to spend time cosying up,' Sister Gregory said, nudging the door inwards, revealing an odious portal to nowhere. 'You can do so in there.' The door's hinges whined; a slow agonising sound that was absorbed by the void beyond, amplifying the girls' fear. 'Go on, get in.' Using the threatening length of Mr Birchwood, Sister Gregory gestured to the vacuous nothingness. Her face was indefinable; eyes and mouth smudges of blackness, like pits of loose earth in which insects and worms crawled and slithered. The white band of coif around her head and the strip of collar at her neck were dirty grey in the gloom. Much too unholy to thwart the darkness.

Neither Maureen nor Jeanette moved. A fusty smell of

age and disuse seeped from the unknown space before them. It could be a cupboard, Maureen supposed, or a vast open hall. It was impossible to tell. They both stood gawping, hands clenched together.

'Or would you prefer it if one of you goes in alone while the other goes elsewhere for a long soak in an ice-cold bath?' Sister Gregory suggested. When neither girl answered, she flicked her wrist – expertly, deftly, precisely – and Mr Birchwood struck the back of Maureen's bare legs.

Stinging agony exploded behind Maureen's eyes, but she caught the pain between clenched teeth, holding it there, uncomfortably quietened, behind her lips. Beetles clicked within the black spaces of her head. She wouldn't give Sister Gregory the satisfaction of crying out. Not doubting for a second that the demented matriarch would carry out her threat to split them up if she didn't act soon, she stepped forward and pulled Jeanette with her into the uncharted space, where they were quickly swallowed by a darkness so heavy it was substantial enough to press down on them with a firm pressure. Their fingers remained interwoven, palms squeezed tightly together.

'How long do we have to stay here?' Jeanette whimpered, too scared to weigh up the potential penalty for speaking out with such boldness.

'As long as it takes, impudent swine,' Sister Gregory said. Mr Birchwood's tip remained on the floor, resting. She leant inside and drew the door towards her, closing it teasingly slowly. 'In the meantime, you'd better pray Tom Dockin doesn't come for you.'

Jeanette whimpered.

Sister Gregory cackled; a noise that excited all the things that might be in the dark with them. Everything imagined stirred. 'First, he'll peel off your skin with his teeth, then he'll drink the blood from your veins and grind your bones between his metal jaws.' Her lipless mouth was a black gash over which her tongue swiped. 'He'll gobble you up, little pigs. One at a time.'

The door clapped shut then, sealing Maureen and Jeanette in an abyss where the wind was barely audible and anything at all might exist. The thunk of the key turning in the lock announced their imprisonment. Both girls, delirious with fear, clutched at each other's arms and listened to the retreating footsteps of Sister Gregory, till there was nothing but the roaring buzz of uncertainty and the quickness of their own breathing.

Maureen scrunched her toes into the cold floor and squeezed her eyes shut against the room's obscurity.

Mary had a little lamb, Mary had a little lamb, Mary had a little lamb.

At times such as this, in her head, she was Mary clutching a fleecy newborn. It was a perception of comfort and love and roused in her a desire to protect. In turn, this lent her a sense (no matter how false or small) of braveness. She hadn't considered that the lamb was an extension of herself.

'Do you think he'll come?' Jeanette asked.

The lamb almost slipped from Maureen's arms. 'No,' she said, heart thumping. Though she thought he would.

Tom Dockin was the bogeyman, a folkloric figure who was said to visit Eden House often, perhaps even lived there. He'd eaten no one during Maureen and Jeanette's stay. Not that they were aware. But then, how could they know for sure?

Timothy Forbes, a troubled twelve-year-old who'd been at Eden House for much longer than Maureen and Jeanette, was missing the thumb and forefinger from his right hand. Whatever had happened, the nuns insisted it was an apt punishment. Meted out by Tom Dockin or misadventure, though, it was unclear. Timothy refused to offer specific details when asked. In fact, he clammed up and devolved into a state of deep trauma whenever anyone brought up the topic of his absent digits. It was, therefore, too easy to think Tom Dockin had chewed them off. It made for a better story. Besides, Dockin had metal teeth, all the better for crunching flesh and bone. And Maureen knew this to be true. He lurked in the shadows, grating his teeth together as though his mouth couldn't be stilled, creating a metallic *snip snip snip* which the building might claim as its own. But she knew he was there. She'd seen his massive shoulders inventing angles where there should be none. Sister Gregory reckoned his eyes glowed red. But whenever Maureen saw him, they were always white, rolled back in his head. Seemingly blind, Dockin was always watching.

Sixteen-year-old Sharon Banks, who shared the same dormitory as Maureen and Jeanette, reckoned he might be the Devil himself. She said the name Dockin was close enough to Dickens and Dickens meant 'devil' and Eden House was definitely somewhere the Devil would feel at home. It made sense to Maureen that that's who the bogeyman might be. But then, maybe Tom Dockin was under no guise at all. What if he was nothing but a glorified bad man with cannibal tendencies and metal teeth? Albeit one who could metamorphose from night time shadows.

'There's no such thing as the bogeyman,' Maureen said.

They both knew she was lying.

Still clinging to Jeanette, she backed up against the door and together they slid down to the draughty floor, where they sat shuddering. Maureen scrunched her eyes shut.

Mary had a little lamb and its fleece was snow and everywhere that Mary went it was white and Mary's lamb was Mary's lamb and its fleece was sure to go.

'What's that noise?' Jeanette said.

Maureen stilled the nonsensical words in her head and listened. 'What noise?'

'Someone else is here with us.'

Then Maureen heard it: a scraping on the wall.

Fingernails on plaster?

Someone drawing closer.

'Who's there?' Maureen's voice was jagged but shrill.

No one answered.

'We aren't scared of you, whoever you are,' she thought to add.

The scratching stopped, as if whoever it was might respond to that claim.

No one did.

A new weighty silence stretched on, making the surrounding emptiness seem somehow smaller. Claustrophobic, perhaps. They were in a well of unfathomable fear in which anything might happen to them. Anything at all. Because anything can exist in the dark, even things that are unimaginable. With this realisation, a new sound presented itself: a metallic gnashing. Rhythmic and deliberate. A chattering of metal against metal.

Teeth against teeth?

Jeanette gripped Maureen's arms so hard Maureen yipped. Then the sound of shuffling marked the approach of whoever was there with them.

Was that the clip of hooves on wood?

For everyone knows the Devil has cloven hooves.

A rough yet wispy snigger, perhaps?

Maureen's entire body was pained with fear. A fear so resolute, she thought her heart might stop and she would die. The lamb had scarpered. She'd lost it to the dark.

'Is it him?' Jeanette said with a sob. Seconds later a wet warmth spread across the cold, hard floor, soaking into Maureen's nightdress.

Maureen closed her eyes and felt her own bladder twinge. 'Yes,' she said. 'I think it might be.'

2

Catherine Hall

2019

A dusting of snow had fallen during the night, but the A171 across the moors was passable and the traffic free-flowing. It was a grey, frosty day; entirely appropriate for mourning. The sort of day that a ship like *Demeter* might wash ashore with crates of soil containing deadly passengers.

I have crossed oceans of time to find you.

My heart was already aching for all the fantasies I'd ever allowed to let breathe and grow inside myself. Mostly these illusions had been borne of too much time spent standing on cliff tops alone, looking at the grey North Sea while thinking melancholy thoughts that I, Catherine Hall, might be akin to Coppola's Count Dracula's Elisabeta, and that my destined love some day would find me. If it turned out he was a monster, as Dracula had been, so be it. He'd be my monster. Romantic and lustful. I lived in foolish hope.

I am longing to be with you, and by the sea, where we can talk together freely and build our castles in the air.

As soon as the ruins of Whitby Abbey came into view in the far distance, with a backdrop of choppy, *Demeter*-less North Sea and winter-bound sky, a tingling sensation as sharp as electricity and as frightening as the hands of my imagined lover coursed over my skin. I shivered. The journey felt like a homecoming, in that I was returning to the only place I'd ever belonged. But this time seemed very much different to the countless other times I'd made the trip. This time I couldn't imagine leaving again; the idea was too much of a malignant threat, pervading the space all around me, thinning the air so I could barely breathe. Whitby's winter would absorb me, I thought. Make me fit its hard edges and bleak colours. Never let go. Grind the life in me till I blended with the grit of every cement-grey tourist thoroughfare. Till no one noticed me at all.

This premonition gripped me with such alarming force that I came over all lightheaded and contemplated pulling over. But then, just as quickly as it had arrived, the strange perception faded in intensity and by the time I was nearing the West Cliff, passing Pannett Park on the right, the boiling pot of nostalgia within me returned to a gentle simmer. I could leave Whitby any time I wanted, I reminded myself. And the vague flash of terror that I was driving to my death (!) seemed nothing but a silly notion. No more substantial than the hands of my lover.

The past was the past, the future unwritten.

I noticed a wilted bouquet secured to a rusted railing at the side of the road, flapping against its bonds in the wind, trying to break free. The sentiment of its placement had dulled to obscurity between curled, brown-edged petals and dirty yellow ribbon. Someone's recent tribute. Someone else's eye-sore. I thought about my mother and the flowers I'd lain by her freshly covered grave. Cream roses. Probably not her favourite. I wondered if they were withering already. I expected so.

It was mid-December. There was nowhere near the same amount of touristy hustle and bustle that crowded the streets during summer months. I found a parking spot right outside The Zoltan and congratulated myself after teasing the car into it with a tight parallel park. Aunt

Lyrica had been living at and running The Zoltan on Whitby's West Cliff since before I was born. Her husband, Ged Black, an older man by about twenty years, had bought the three-storey B&B establishment some time in the seventies, about eight years and a failed marriage before he'd met then married Aunt Lyrica.

Built in the late Victorian era for a sea captain, the house is a red-brick building with a pointed apex to the front and a red-tiled canopy above the main door which makes a perfect shelter from the rain. The Zoltan had maintained significant kerb appeal. As a kid I remember thinking it looked like a small palace. Regarding it now, as I switched off the car engine, I still thought so.

Inside there is a jumble of hallways, stairs and rooms. A layout of which I'll never tire. There are eight guest rooms in total; four twin, three double and a single. All of them en suite, apart from the single which has use of a small private bathroom across the landing on the second floor. Over the years I've jumped on every bed in every room and studied the view from every window. It's like a well-loved puzzle. One I can put in a box and store away till the next time I visit. Its pieces worn and pliant in my fingers, hugely pleasing to my wistful sensibilities – the colours, the textures, the way I think I remember something, but don't. Each time I return to The Zoltan, I can't wait to tip the pieces out of the box again. To splay them around. Slot them together. As with every old puzzle, sometimes I find the odd piece missing.

As soon as he'd taken it over, Uncle Ged changed the name of the B&B from West Cliff Eskape (a wordplay on the River Esk which flows through Whitby into the North Sea) to The Zoltan (Dracula's dog, the slavering Doberman in the 1978 movie *Zoltan... Hound of Dracula)*. Anyone not up to scratch on horror trivia might assume the namesake to be some mysterious, olive-skinned, seafaring adventurer with good looks, white harem trousers, a clipped black beard and a plucky spirit – a bit like Sinbad. But really it's a ferocious, territorial, vampiric hell-hound – a bit like depression.

Okay, okay, so that might sound like a strange analogy. Let me explain. I mean, I can't know for certain, since he's no longer around to confirm my theory, but I reckon Uncle Ged named the B&B with some sort of symbolism in mind. He was a multi-layered man, probably searched for meaning and metaphor in just about anything. Same as Aunt Lyrica. I like to think The Zoltan was a metaphor for the black dog of depression, subliminally hidden behind an exotic-sounding name.

Make any more sense yet?

No?

All right. Well, Uncle Ged would have expected (wanted) holidaymakers to arrive at the B&B and to let their black dogs loose on the beach while they enjoyed nice walks along the promenade with fish and chips, ice-cream cones and candy floss. Then after however many nights at The Zoltan, when it was time to head home, they could leave their black dogs behind. It's a beguiling analogy, if I have it right. At least, I think so. I only wish he'd thought to hang a sign at the door to prove my theory: 'Black dogs welcome! Feel free to leave them here.'

Maybe I'm a million miles off the mark though. I dunno. I hope not. All I know is that The Zoltan has appeased my black dog plenty over the years.

As an adult I reckon I understand Uncle Ged more. That my perception of him, of how I like to imagine he would have mentally processed things, is accurate. But then again, perhaps I've glorified him in my head. Become absorbed by his character too much, so I don't know what's him and what's me anymore. He's the only man I've ever been close to. The only man I've ever loved. When I say that, I mean in the unconditional sense of how you'd love a family member. Like how I love Aunt

Lyrica. And how I'd love a god if I believed in one.

As a kid I spent every memorable minute of every school holiday at The Zoltan, even when Uncle Ged was no longer around. Aunt Lyrica had been a surrogate mother of sorts since before I can remember, and I'd assumed the role of her surrogate daughter when Calanthe left. Therefore, the day after the funeral of my biological mother it seemed like the natural thing to do: to make the hour-long journey to stay with Aunt Lyrica.

3

Lyrica Black

2019

'Cat's coming to stay for a while.' There was no one else in the kitchen, but Lyrica didn't feel alone. Often talked to empty rooms. 'Isn't that great?'

The hum of the oven's fan and the rattle of a car engine somewhere further along Crescent Avenue was the only response. A shadow grazed the wall. Lyrica barely noticed. She lined a baking tray with grease-proof paper, then set out six neat circles of dough, evenly spaced. She was the calmest she'd been in days. Didn't keep worrying her face with her fingers or biting her thumbs till they were bleeding and sore. Catherine was on her way to The Zoltan. A welcome, much needed distraction.

Since the death of her sister over a week ago, something malignant within the spaces of Lyrica which she'd have preferred left unprovoked grew bigger. A deep, dark, festering lagoon of fear filled with snakes and insects. Not a day went by where she didn't hear lithe bodies slithering inside the walls and the *tick-tick-tick* of many arthropod feet echoing within the structure of The Zoltan. She imagined if she didn't seize the opportunity to do some emotional sorting they'd eat the structural innards till the whole building collapsed around her, then from out of the rubble the bogeyman would crawl to drag her into his depravity.

Together, she hoped she and Catherine might shuffle

through this initial stage of loss. Determine how they felt about things. Conclude what ghosts, if any, lived within the walls.

The Zoltan used to be a safe place. A sturdy stronghold of happy memories which her husband Ged had helped build and defend. But on the day of his funeral, over twenty years ago, old terrors from Eden House caught up with Lyrica. Her sister brought them along to the wake. And ever since they'd lurked in the guesthouse's corners and shadows. Had probably affected Calanthe more than Lyrica liked to admit. Perhaps Catherine too.

For this, Lyrica harboured regret – and a slight bitterness towards her sister for having brought the past into the present. Both of their girls had deserved nothing less than carefree childhoods, but that's not how it panned out. Far from it. Calanthe was lost, hadn't even reached adulthood before vanishing one evening some time between the setting of the sun and the rising of the moon. She'd left all of her belongings behind and a scorched memory of the person she'd been. No trace of her ever found. She was a radiant light forever mourned. As for Catherine, she seemed lost within her own mind most of the time. Held too many insecurities. An unstable childhood, despite Lyrica's best efforts to make it as normal as possible, had left her with whatever mental traumas she suffered. Lyrica couldn't say how deep her niece's emotional injuries ran, but suspected those traumas had caused substantial and irreversible damage. The way Catherine behaved around others reflected this. Her awkwardness. The way she found it hard to bond. To trust. To love.

That Catherine was coming to stay thrilled Lyrica. She craved interactive company, because even though she saw plenty of guests coming and going throughout the year, winter months could be especially lonely at The Zoltan. Too many dark hours. Too much time to think, to go over all the things that had and hadn't happened. To obsess over all the choices made that led to this point. And to fret about all the things that might exist in the shadows. Because lately Lyrica imagined she could make out the sound of someone creeping about in unoccupied guestrooms and corridors at night. A faint swishing of black fabric, inciting unwelcome nightmares. And she was sure she'd seen the bogeyman skulking in dark corners and blind spots. Had detected the heaviness of his form shifting from room to room, his hooves brushing across the carpet. The clang of old pipes settling in the night always concealed his rattling breaths. But he did that on purpose. Subtle signs, enough to let her know he was there, but vague enough to make her doubt her sanity. The devil was in the detail.

Did Catherine remember Tom Dockin?

It would be impossible for Lyrica to know unless she came out and asked the question. But she didn't think it necessary or wise to broach the subject on the off-chance her niece had successfully repressed the memory. Catherine and Calanthe had been just ten years old at the time of Ged's funeral. So young and impressionable. The last thing Lyrica wanted was to poke at the tenuous membrane of whatever denial Catherine might have put in place to protect her sanity.

So Lyrica decided that unless Catherine mentioned Tom Dockin, there'd be no talk of him.

If no one talked about him, then he didn't exist. That's what Ged had told her often. It was a good coping strategy, one that had given her many years of relative peace. But Ged's death had left Lyrica temporarily vulnerable, and that's when her sister had brought all the hellishness of the past right to her front door and into her home. Shapes and nightmares had grown in the shadows, building in weight and tenacity. And even after Calanthe disappeared, the shadows had stayed, lingering at The

Zoltan, festering like an infection. There was dread in every dark space and unseen room. A spiteful hint of the depravity of something just out of reach, never fully in sight. But it was there. Existing. And now, following her sister's death, the shadows were that little blacker and wider and taller each night. The bugs and snakes and insurmountable trepidation that Tom Dockin was around every corner were back. Lyrica told herself it was owing to her subconscious digging around in the past. But deep down she had a niggling sense that something bad was building. That something categorically awful would happen. Which is why she needed Catherine around, to help stabilise the manic thoughts spiralling out of control and make her realise she was being altogether too paranoid.

A woodlouse wriggled from behind the nearby bread bin and scuttled across the counter, much too close to her batch of scones. It was a repugnant thing. Didn't belong in the kitchen. Lyrica was more fearful than disgusted by its presence though. It belonged in some other place, some other time. Not here, not now. She swiped it to the floor with the back of her hand. Wanted it gone. A surge of satisfaction rose in her when she stamped down and felt its armour crunch beneath her foot.

But then…

If there was one, how many more would infiltrate the spaces in her home? All of them creeping around in places they shouldn't be.

Don't wallow in the past, Lyrica warned, gripping the edge of the counter. There's nothing but terror behind you.

On cue, a sizeable shadow flashed across the wall in her peripheral vision.

She spun round.

No one was there.

She heard Sister Gregory's grizzly voice in the confines

of her head: First, he'll peel off your skin with his teeth. The nun's rotten words were bound in the intricately preserved memories Lyrica kept of Eden House like truths she'd rather not know. Secrets she was too ashamed to share.

Then he'll drink the blood from your veins.

Lyrica grabbed for a glass tumbler and filled it with water, then downed almost half in one go.

And then he'll grind your bones between his metal jaws.

'But he didn't,' Lyrica said to the empty kitchen, her eyes flashing manically triumphant. 'He came, but he didn't eat us.'

Sister Gregory laughed. Are you sure about that, little pig?

4

Catherine Hall

2019

The North Sea air sliced through my clothes, whipped my hair about and stung my bare hands till my fingers and knuckles turned an unattractive shade of purple. I set my suitcase on the kerb, then looked up at The Zoltan's third floor apex. Orange-red bricks simmered against a snow-churning grey sky. Hanging on the front door was a festive wreath decorated with pine cones and red berries. Fa-la-la-la-la. The door swung inwards. Aunt Lyrica was standing in the entrance vestibule. Must have been waiting for me, watching out of the window.

'Here she is. Here's my little Cat,' she called.

Aunt Lyrica is an inch or two shorter than me and about fourteen pounds lighter, yet sometimes she still calls me 'little Cat.' Old habits die hard, I guess. She was my mother's sister, divided by a mere eleven and a half months. Apparently they'd been close at some point. Not that they weren't in recent years, they'd just drifted apart the way adults do when families and responsibilities grow. Aunt Lyrica hadn't bothered travelling north for the funeral. I didn't know why and had no interest in asking. She has her own way of doing things, especially when it comes to dealing with loss. I trust she made the right choice for herself.

She greeted me with an empathic smile at the doorstep

and pulled me into a bone-scrunching hug. Her burgundy hair, drawn into a messy bun, tickled my cheek. She smelt of patchouli, as ever, and was predominantly dressed in black – not with any specific mourning in mind for my mother, I dare say, but just because she loves black. At least one part of her outfit is almost always made of crushed velvet. Today it was her top; a figure-hugging bodice which laced up the front, crested by pale cleavage, and was the only thing that wasn't black. Instead, it was some wistfully romantic colour that lay somewhere between pink and purple. Like the underbelly of a dragon that rides the sky at sunset.

'How was the journey, love?' Aunt Lyrica asked. Her large blue eyes, highlighted with charcoal makeup, were only faintly marred by subtle lines of age. At fifty-two she was attractive. But then, she always had been. A guaranteed head-turner with a witchy air of mystery and a contagious laugh that rendered most men – and lots of women – spellbound. She's the kind of woman songs are written about.

I was twenty years younger than Aunt Lyrica. Still very much in my prime, whatever that's supposed to mean. But I considered myself disgustingly plain and dowdy in comparison.

'Not bad,' I said, looking beyond her into the hallway where The Zoltan beckoned me to step into its familiar maze of rooms and memories.

Welcome home.

Aunt Lyrica reached down to take the handle of my suitcase, but I swatted her hand away and dragged it up onto the doorstep. 'It's okay.' I trailed it behind me into the hallway. 'I've got it.'

Aunt Lyrica closed the front door, sealing out any wintry blasts of sea air that might think to follow us. The Zoltan radiated a cosy warmth from the entrance radiator, which instantly made my nose run. I sniffled. Felt my body relax. Joss sticks and festive spices filled the place with familiarity.

Perhaps at the end the little things may teach us most.

Perhaps.

'Let's get your stuff to your room first, shall we?' Aunt Lyrica said. 'Then we can catch up.' She brushed past me and headed towards the stairs.

I fished a paper hanky from my pocket, wiped my nose, then followed. From behind, Aunt Lyrica's waist looked tiny. My entire torso was like a tree trunk. Or an elephant's leg. I lacked all the curves and feminine lines of the other Hall women – Aunt Lyrica, my mother and my half-sister, Summer. Calanthe, too.

Doctor, you don't know what it is to doubt everything, even yourself.

Especially yourself.

My suitcase was heavy, but I heaved it upwards. Didn't make a big deal of it. I imagined that instead of my jeans, hoodies, underwear and toiletries, it contained the desiccated body of a vampire whom I might revive with plenty of good cheer and a holly-jolly Christmas attitude. If I moped too much, it would disintegrate into black ashes and The Zoltan would set all the black dogs it had ever kept in its midst upon me.

'So far, there's only one room booked out this week,' Aunt Lyrica said. 'So I thought we may as well spread out. You can have your own, bigger space.'

The alternative would have been to use the spare room in the ground floor living quarters right next to Aunt Lyrica's bedroom; it used to be Calanthe's room. I'd slept there countless times, even in the post Calanthe years, but was always happier, given the choice, to take a guest room at The Zoltan during quiet spells. The ghost of Calanthe could be quite oppressive.

'Sounds great,' I said.

The third stair from the top creaked beneath my weight,

as I expected it would. My chest filled with a feeling I can only describe as contentment and, whether fickle or not, at this feeling of contentment the vampire in my suitcase fleshed out a little. The wizened muscle that was its deadened, bloodthirsty heart pulsed once, maybe twice. I set my case down on the landing and sighed.

'I'm pleased you came.' Aunt Lyrica turned her head and smiled.

Me too.

She was the only family I had left, apart from Summer. But Summer had Patrick and, therefore, no real need for me. Besides, too many years divided us, and too many other factors that I won't go into.

Patrick's Summer's dad, by the way. I never had one of my own. I realise there must have been a man who contributed to the making of me, I just didn't know who. My mother gave me her surname at birth and that's all there was to it. Growing up, I remember thinking my biological father was more of a mystery than Santa Claus. And now he'd remain forever that way because my mother had taken his identity to the grave. This left me with a bitter aftertaste of resentment which seared my chest like heartburn. No matter how terrible, shameful or disreputable the story of my conception might be, I felt my mother owed me at least my father's name. Because without that detail, I knew I'd never be whole. I'd always seem like half of whatever. Mediocre in every way. Catherine Hall: too dull to be brilliant, but too competent to be wholly insignificant. Half of me missing.

Even Patrick Hill didn't want me. I was fourteen when my mother met him. He already had a daughter with his first wife, then he and my mother had Summer not long after their marriage. There was no real reason for him to be interested in me. Together they formed the perfect family unit. I was the odd one out. The only Hall in a house of Hills; an 'a' and an 'i' was all the difference between me and them. But oh what a difference it made.

My mother once said that I could take on Patrick's surname if I wanted. I didn't. And thankfully no one ever suggested it again. I wasn't a Hill. It was the name from a branch of a family tree whose blood or love would never belong to me. Besides, Summer had already peaked the Hill. She would forever stand at the top, basking in the sun. If I was to become a Hill, I'd always be climbing, never reaching the summit.

Whether I liked it or not, I was definitely a Hall. Inside me were many echoes. Instead of fancy tables and chairs, chandeliers and gold-framed paintings, there was a small invisible cat, the ghost of a beautiful blonde girl, a snake entwined skull and a velvety witch.

'Thought I'd put you in here,' Aunt Lyrica said, guiding me along the first floor landing and into Room One – a spacious double with Victoriana-chic flocked wallpaper in cream and taupe swirls and an old fireplace feature stacked with church candles. A sumptuous, burgundy throw and four fat pillows covered the bed. Expensive curtains in a shade of deoxygenated blood framed the window and looked heavy enough to keep out chills at night – and light during the day to keep my ailing vampire from ruin. Dark red trimmings and accessories complemented the room. It was perfect. Just perfect.

My stomach growled with a pang of emptiness, which made me blush and Aunt Lyrica laugh.

'Hungry by any chance, love?' she said, with a wink.

Nodding (because how could I not?) I clutched a hand to my belly and felt the soft roundedness of it hanging over the waistband of my jeans. The last thing I'd eaten was a corned beef slice at my mother's wake the day before. Patrick had arranged the spread. He'd arranged everything, in fact. The coffin, flowers, transport and hymns. Not once had I seen him cry. Summer had cried enough for them both. For the entire day she'd been like a fragile flower head clinging to the sturdy stem of her youth while the death of Mother hit her in stormy blasts of grief.

Poor Summer.

I'd kept my distance. Didn't want to impinge on her and Patrick's display of father/daughter shared sorrow. Patrick had put his sturdy, protective arm around Summer's shoulders many times and hadn't strayed far from her side. I, on the other hand, had sat in the corner farthest away from the buffet table, where I was patted and fussed over by my mother's best friend Sheila. It was Sheila who'd brought me a half of lager from the bar, not Patrick. And Sheila who'd accompanied me, paper plate and napkin in hand, to the buffet queue.

When I'd set off on my journey to Whitby that morning, I hadn't had breakfast and, false mawkishness aside, it hadn't seemed appropriate to eat something as cold and meaningless as a sandwich bought from the petrol station. I'd thought it only right to fast until presented with Aunt Lyrica's food, because then it would be okay, for the sake of the stickler side of me that enjoys formality, to eat again, to follow up on Mother's funeral spread.

'Come on then, little Cat,' Aunt Lyrica said, patting me on the arm and jostling me onto the landing. 'I made some cheese scones especially. They'll still be warm.'

I felt the vampire in my suitcase unfurl a little. Its lungs inflated the tiniest bit and its heart beat stronger than the last time.

I was back where I belonged.

5

Catherine Hall

2019

'I'm sorry I couldn't be there for you yesterday,' Aunt Lyrica said, taking a seat at the dining table opposite me. In the space between us there was a chunky wooden bread board with four cheese scones on top, a butter knife and a cream ceramic butter dish with hand-painted pink roses on its glazed surface.

I shrugged, didn't want to talk about the funeral. Not yet. Maybe never.

'It's okay.' I wafted a hand. 'Don't worry about it.'

Aunt Lyrica poured us tea from a teapot shaped like the Cheshire Cat from *Alice in Wonderland*. Its yellow eyes stared madly at me as steam and tea spewed from its nose. 'How's Summer?'

'With Patrick.'

'Hmmm.' Aunt Lyrica cocked an eyebrow at my abstruse response. 'And you?' Her dark blue eyes fixed on mine, as if daring me to not answer straight this time. She set the teapot on the table. 'Like, *really*. How are you?'

'Fine. Really. I'm fine.' Without being invited to tuck in, I reached for a scone. I needed something to do. A task to focus on. Didn't want the awkwardness of emotion to fill up all the space in the kitchen with such a weighty air I could no longer move. 'We knew it was coming, didn't we? It was a blessing in the end.'

Aunt Lyrica looked surprised. Then her face relaxed when she realised I was merely spewing empty sentiments as people are wont to do in such circumstances. 'Still, it wasn't fair,' she said.

'What is?' I shrugged. 'Besides, she did it to herself.'

Again, that shocked expression. 'She needed help.'

Who doesn't? 'At least she's at peace now.'

'I hope so.' Aunt Lyrica didn't seem convinced by the possibility. She watched as I cut the scone in half with the knife and helped myself to butter from the dish. Her eyes were glassy, but I doubted she'd cry. 'She loved you, you know.'

I nibbled at the edge of the still-warm savoury treat, feigning politeness. Such table-side manners weren't required of me here, but still it didn't stop me refraining from cramming the whole crumbly wedge in my mouth. I made a noise that could have passed as either appreciation towards Aunt Lyrica's culinary skills or an affirmative response to her remark.

'It was hard for her back then,' Aunt Lyrica persisted, making the statement sound more like a question. I realised then I couldn't dodge this line of conversation. She wanted more from me. Was reeling me in. Therapy, perhaps? Did she hope to fix whatever it was she thought broken inside of me? Was she about to tell me what had kept my mother from truly loving me? Or was she simply trying to tell me that things had been a lot harder for my mother than I'd ever known?

I took a deep breath and said, 'When I was born, you mean?'

'Yes.' Aunt Lyrica continued to watch me eat, making no attempt to take any food for herself. 'Before you were born as well. It was hard for us both.'

'What happened?'

'Too much.'

'She never talked about the past.'

'No, I can't imagine why she would have.'

I expected Aunt Lyrica to say more. When she didn't, I said, 'Will you tell me?'

'I'm not sure either of us is ready for that. Nor if we ever will be.' Aunt Lyrica sipped at her tea. 'You stayed here a lot, not because your mother didn't want you, just…'

'Just what?'

'She was in a bad place.'

I looked around at the kitchen walls and the hotchpotch of crockery, utensils and appliances that cluttered the surface of the oak units. This was Aunt Lyrica's usual chaos, every single bit of it. Even down to the aroma of fresh-baked food mingled with her patchouli scent. My favourite memories by far were those of being with her at The Zoltan, not with my mother. I took up the second half of buttered scone and bit into it. 'At least I wasn't.'

Aunt Lyrica smiled through a frown. 'Ged was always good with you kids. You could have been ours, you know.'

'I know.' And I did. I'd spent my entire life wishing I was. I held all the memories I had of Uncle Ged close to my heart. He'd been an ear-studded, bearded father figure with kind eyes and a warm laugh, enriched by the many rollies he'd smoked over the years. His fingertips had been stained yellow from his tobacco addiction and his knuckles adorned with the smudged dark green outlines of tattoos that were probably as old as Aunt Lyrica. Not a day had gone by where he hadn't worn blue denim jeans and black t-shirts with some ensemble of skulls and roses and snakes on them. His favourite music was heavy metal. I remember him bouncing me on his knee in time to Motörhead's *Ace of Spades* when I was about four. I always considered myself safe with Uncle Ged. He had large hands and a gruff, manly voice.

Along with heavy metal, motorbikes and baking, Uncle

Ged loved horror fiction. He had three large bookcases, rammed with paperbacks. The creased white-worn spines of black covers displayed names such as James Herbert, Stephen King and Dean Koontz; the usual crew. He also had a hardback edition of Bram Stoker's *Dracula*, of which he was particularly fond, given that the story is partly based in Whitby itself. Bound in black leather, silver foil flourishes decorated the book's front cover. It was a delight to hold, to run your fingers over. I remember Calanthe and I devoured its pages as soon as we were old enough to understand their content. In fact, it became Calanthe's bible. Perhaps mine too.

Not only did he teach me how to read, Uncle Ged was the one who'd removed the stabilisers from my bike. I can still picture the scene: it was a warm, summer evening, right outside The Zoltan. He'd gripped my shoulders as I'd balanced on two wheels for that first terrifying time. Then strode behind me as my feet worked the pedals, his right hand planted between my shoulder blades because I'd told him 'don't let go'. When we got halfway along Crescent Avenue, he'd pushed me on my way and cheered. Petrified at first because he wasn't keeping me upright, I'd squealed. The blast of the otherwise still air rushing into my face, swishing my hair over my shoulders, and the thought I'd fall off at any moment and land in a painful, tangled mess with the bike's metal frame was overwhelming. But when I didn't fall and when Uncle Ged continued to cheer me on, I felt special. Like I'd done something clever and momentous like landing on the moon. Perhaps it sounds sad, piteous even, but it's one of the best memories I have.

'You were like twins, you and Calanthe,' Aunt Lyrica said.

'We looked nothing alike.'

'Your personalities weren't anything alike either, but you went everywhere together.'

Not everywhere, I thought.

'I swear I can sense her sometimes.' Aunt Lyrica looked more wistful than she had before. There was a dark seriousness behind her eyes which I thought must be linked to death. Or something as irreversible.

A shiver coursed through me and the vampire in my case became still. Its heart stopped beating. 'How do you mean?'

'I think she's here. Like, she's not out there living this other life somewhere else as we'd supposed. I think she's… dead. Only, she's not moved on like your Uncle Ged did.'

'You can't be sure of that.'

'But it's what I feel. And I'm not sure what to do. Just listen for her, Cat. See if she'll talk to you.'

I nodded. 'Okay.' If Calanthe was around, then perhaps she would, if she was able. I wet my finger and collected the crumbs from my plate, transferring them to my mouth. 'You're the only person who ever calls me Cat, you know.'

Aunt Lyrica brushed a stray strand of hair behind her ear. Her face was bone-white, almost flawless. 'Does it bother you?'

'No.' I shook my head. 'Makes me feel like someone else.' And that's fine, I thought, because I'm not Catherine Hall. Or maybe I am. I dunno. It's simply the name my mother assigned me at birth, like a brand to be shaped and evolved throughout my life. My identifier. It's the name that's printed in faded black Courier typeface on my birth certificate. Two nouns which depict different personal and visual connotations to anyone who ever knew or met me. The other names on my birth certificate, in the same typewritten font, are Jeanette Hall, my mother, and Mary Lansdale, the registrar.

The sound of a person's name, the way it rolls off the tongue, whether that be harsh, soft, unusual or ordinary, has some initial and lasting bearing on how a person is subconsciously perceived by others. That's the way with names. And we never get to choose them for ourselves, not in the beginning anyway. Not when it matters most. We develop our names over time with our mere existence and whatever impact we have on those around us.

The name Catherine is associated with the Greek word katharos, meaning 'pure'. Pure what though? It always seemed like a trap laid out by my mother for me to prove. Or to determine what it is I'm not contaminated by. I wonder if when she looked at me for the first time she imagined (or hoped) that I'd be pure of heart. It's a term I've heard other people use more than once or twice in my lifetime. Not about me specifically, I might add, though I'm not even sure what it means. And besides, I don't believe I'm anything at all in its purest form.

Are any of us?

My younger sister, Summer, is everything you'd expect her to be: stunning, vibrant and confident. She defines 'summer' to a tee. It was the same with my cousin, Calanthe. Calanthe means 'beautiful flower'. It's a type of orchid. Coupled with her surname Black, Calanthe was destined from the beginning to be exotic and mysterious.

Aunt Lyrica took another sip of her drink. Her smoky eyes were unyielding and mesmeric. 'Why don't you reinvent yourself? Become someone else.'

'Like you did, you mean?'

Aunt Lyrica pondered my question, then nodded. 'I never wanted to be Maureen Hall. Especially after everything that happened at Eden House.'

Eden House, now there was a place rarely mentioned. Bereavement must have shaken it loose from the bonds Aunt Lyrica kept it shackled with. At the behest of grief caused by my mother's death, it had risen to the surface. Slipped right out into the open like a dirty word spoken in polite company.

'Will you tell me what happened there?'

Aunt Lyrica sat back in her chair and looked to the ceiling. Usually she had a good poker face, but I could see the pain lodged within her as clearly as I could see she was my mother's sister.

'No,' she said after some deliberation.

'Okay.' Today wasn't the day I'd learn anything more about Eden House. No meant no. It wasn't up for debate. Never was. But that didn't stop me trying to spark a debate now and then. 'Why did you choose Lyrica?'

Aunt Lyrica sat forward again and rested her elbows on the table, her expression less guarded already. Less haunted. 'It sounded right in my head. I like to think I'm quite lyrical. It represents me well.'

'Do you think Catherine represents me well?'

'Only you can decide that.'

'You mustn't think so, you only ever call me Cat.'

'I love cats more than most things. It suits you.'

'You don't have a cat.'

Aunt Lyrica shrugged. 'Kevin doesn't like them.'

We both looked to the black wire-haired Patterdale terrier who was curled up in a dog bed by the radiator. He was old and grumpy and blissfully unaware that he was being talked about.

'Why didn't you get a cat instead?' I asked.

'Because then I wouldn't have Kevin, would I?' Aunt Lyrica made a face to suggest I was being absurd. 'We can't have everything we want.'

I took another scone and tore it in two with my fingers. 'You never shortened Calanthe's name.'

'That's true.'

'You don't call Summer by anything else either.'

'Summer knows who she is just fine.'

'And Calanthe?'

'Yeah, I think she knew too.'

Really? I wasn't so sure.

I ate half of the second scone, remembering how Calanthe used to call me Wilhelmina. Wilhelmina Murray if she was in a teasing mood. She fancied herself as being Lucy Westenra, the vivacious and wanton stunner from Bram Stoker's *Dracula* who had all the men falling over themselves to get to her. She thought it was funny that I was plain and seemingly straitlaced in comparison, which is why she nicknamed me Wilhelmina Murray – after Lucy Westenra's conservative best friend, Mina. Ever since those days I've longed for someone like the Count to see the appeal beneath my Wilhelmina façade. For him to love me for all that I am; harsh lines and plainness. For him show me a passion worth dying for, his desire alternating from black and ferocious to flesh-coloured and tender. For him to alter time and all reason to reach me if that's what it took.

I have crossed oceans of time to find you.

'I might change my name to Autumn,' I said, at last.

'Now you're being silly.'

'Why? I like Autumn.'

'I'll tell you what's better.'

'What?'

'Spring.'

I inhaled deeply. 'Now you're being silly.'

'Why do you feel you have to live in Summer's shadow?'

'I don't feel that I have to. I just do. That's the way it is.'

'No, it isn't.'

'It is, and that's okay. I love Summer. Everyone does.'

'Everyone loves cats too.'

'Calanthe didn't.'

'No.' Aunt Lyrica looked almost regretful.

There was a long, angry blast from the buzzer in the entrance hall, killing all thoughts of Summer and cats. Rather than a quick, polite beep for attention, whoever was out there kept their finger pressed on the button. Aunt Lyrica stood up, the feet of her chair scraping across the floor. She didn't look at all harassed or irritated by the intrusion. I followed her from the kitchen into the hallway, curious to see who was so bold and arrogant to demand her attention so forcefully. Irritated enough for the pair of us.

At the foot of the stairs by the oak table which accommodated the buzzer (and a guest book and various leaflets and pamphlets about what to do in the area), there was a man, around mid-thirties, wearing a padded black coat and a woollen grey beanie. He had a backpack slung over his right shoulder and carried an SLR camera in his left hand. Immediately I thought I knew him from somewhere else, some other time, but this perception of past acquaintance was so vague it was little more than a mild tugging on my brain.

'Oh hey, you off out for the day?' Aunt Lyrica spoke to the man as though they were good friends.

I stood back and watched them from a distance.

The man smiled, his teeth white and straight. 'Yeah. Sorry to bother you.' He had a Scottish accent, his voice a contradiction of gravelled smoothness, and I thought then I mustn't know him because I'd surely remember that voice. 'I'm going for a walk along the beach. Probably head along to Sandsend, see what pictures I can get.' He waved his camera at Aunt Lyrica in case she might not have seen it already. 'I'm a wee bit concerned about mobile signal when out and about though…'

Aunt Lyrica laughed. 'Ah yes, there are parts of Whitby that still prefer the old ways. Like, before Facebook and what have you. Can't always check-in to let the world know you've just sat down for fish and chips and a pint.'

The man nodded, his blue (stranger's) eyes glinting. 'Anyway, the thing is, my pa's in hospital and I'm worried that if anyone in the family needs to reach me and

I don't have signal… I dunno, would it be okay if I gave your landline number as a backup? Everything should be fine, I imagine, I just worry too much. And I'll only be out for a few hours. I mean, I hate to be a bother…'

Bored with their exchange, I wandered through to the guest dining room where breakfast was served each morning. There were eight compact tables, only one of them made up with clean white linen and cutlery, ready for the following day. Throughout my stay, however long that might be, I'd help Aunt Lyrica to serve whatever variations of the Full English to whatever guests she might have. The following morning it looked set to be only the man in the foyer.

On the chimneybreast wall there was a painting I hadn't seen before. A large crimson rose with a black one behind it, wilted and dying. I stood and stared at the brush strokes till nothing else existed but the red and black blooms.

Life and death.

Blood and ashes.

I am longing to be with you.

The vampire in my suitcase was breathing again, its flesh less papery already. It felt good. But something else breathed within the same space of my imagination. Something not as imagined. Something hidden. Something…

Aunt Lyrica laughed in the hallway and everything around me came rushing back into focus. The Scotsman said something, his voice like peanut brittle. Got stuck in my teeth. I didn't catch the words. 'No worries, have a good day,' Aunt Lyrica called after him. Seconds later she came and found me in the dining room.

'Who was that?' I asked, my head filled with his voice. I had the same inkling as before, that I knew him from some other time. Only, it was more of an uncomfortable sensation now. My innards churned.

'Your neighbour.' Aunt Lyrica smiled, looking years

younger than she had any right to. 'Bloke from Room Two.'

'Oh.'

'Made sense to put him in the room next to yours, so it's more efficient to heat the place.'

'You actively sought to put me next door to a complete stranger?' I went to the window and caught sight of the man with his camera before he rounded the bend of Crescent Avenue and slipped out of view.

'You're staying in a B&B, you silly sod.' Aunt Lyrica shrugged. 'Besides, Dan seems harmless enough.'

It surprised me to hear that she was on first-name terms, though I didn't know why. It was hardly unusual. 'What's his story?'

'No idea.'

'Fair enough. None of my business, I suppose, I'm just a nosy cow.'

'That you are.' Aunt Lyrica's face was deadpan, but her eyes sparked with humour.

'How can you possibly presume to know that he's harmless enough though?'

'I don't suppose I can know for sure, but he has a nice aura about him.'

'Aura?'

'Yeah. You should let yours out more, it's looking grey and shabby.'

'Ah, I get it.' I nodded, still smiling. 'Your aura's been flirting with Dan's.'

'Don't be daft.' Aunt Lyrica rolled her eyes.

'Because you never flirt, do you?'

She ran her hand over the cloth on the made-up table as if to smooth it, even though there were no creases in the fabric. Her eyes glinted with a mischievousness that matched my own. 'Only with loneliness, kidda.'

'And does it ever flirt back?'

Planting both of her hands on the table, she leant

forward, exposing more cleavage, and said, 'Oh, all the time. It's a total slut.'

I laughed; on the surface amused, but deep down knowing just how tragically promiscuous loneliness could be.

'So, do you like my new painting?' Aunt Lyrica straightened up and gestured to the canvas on the chimneybreast.

'I didn't realise you did family portraits.'

She looked at me, bemused. 'Have you been smoking something funny?'

'It's me and Summer.' I moved away from the window to stand in front of the painting. With my open right hand, I drew her attention to the crimson rose and said, 'That's Summer, right there.' Then I pointed to the rose behind. 'And that one, the dead one, that's me.'

Aunt Lyrica exhaled a huff of weary laughter. 'There is no dead one. It's a rose and its shadow, you tit.'

'Looks dead to me.'

'Well, it's not.'

I studied the painting for a while longer. 'There's no way that's a shadow.' I touched the canvas with tentative fingers. 'It's too black. Has too much substance.'

'It's art. *My* art. And I'm telling you it's a bloody shadow.'

'Art's subjective. And I'm telling you it's me and Summer.'

'Well, if that's the case, it could just as easily be me and your mother.'

Interesting. Yes, perhaps just as fitting, I thought. Or it could be me and Calanthe. Only, when I looked at the painting again, I wasn't sure which rose would represent her and which one me.

6

Catherine Hall

2019

I spent the rest of the day with Aunt Lyrica. Not always speaking, just enjoying the time we had together. Breathing the same air, sharing the same rooms. The same blood. We took Kevin for a walk along the West Cliff. He had no real interest in leaving the house; it was too cold out, but Aunt Lyrica put his coat on and insisted he go. For some fresh air and to stretch those old legs, she'd said. And because you've got the yard stinking of piss, buggerlugs, which simply won't do. We took him as far as the whale bones, then decided we weren't as enthusiastic as we'd thought.

'Shall we head back now?' Aunt Lyrica suggested. 'It's bloody freezing.'

'Definitely.' I nodded. Couldn't imagine venturing down to the harbour area, not today. Whitby is all steps and steep banks and my body was too tense to negotiate any of them. The brutal wind was like knife blades being hurled from the North Sea, slicing my exposed face, making parts of it raw and other parts numb. I linked my arm through Aunt Lyrica's and we huddled together, fists clenched, as we turned and fought our way back.

At the change of direction, strands of Aunt Lyrica's hair escaped in long burgundy trails from the collar of her coat. She could easily be Lucy Westenra, I thought. From the film, not the book. Only, properly grownup, like if the Count hadn't given her the fatal kiss of death.

I cast a longing look to the tempestuous grey sea, saw no ships there. Not today.

'How about Mina?' I said, pretending for a moment I looked just as beautiful.

'Who's that?'

'Me?'

Aunt Lyrica's eyes showed quiet amusement. 'Mina Harker?'

'No, Mina Murray. I'm not married. Not even to an accountant.'

Aunt Lyrica laughed. 'Yes, I like Mina. She was intelligent and astute. Mothered all the other characters in *Dracula*. She was a complex woman, the real star of the story.'

'Do you think I'm complex?'

'Definitely.' Aunt Lyrica tugged on Kevin's leader, pulling him away from a patch of grass he was showing too much interest in. 'And there's got to be a Jonathan Harker out there for you somewhere.'

I gripped her arm more tightly and smiled, not sure if I wanted a Jonathan Harker. I'd rather have the Count.

Further along the promenade a man was walking towards us. He was tall and broad, his coat long and black, flapping in the biting wind. The way he moved, taking great strides but not making much progress seemed somehow familiar. Unsettling. I pulled my collar up to shield my neck from the wind and steered Aunt Lyrica across the wide road. Didn't want to cross paths with the man. Didn't want to see his face.

'Is Dan back yet?' I asked.

'Hmmm. Not sure,' Aunt Lyrica said. 'I don't think I noticed him before we left.'

'What about his family? Like, if they ring The Zoltan with news of his dad.'

'Shit, I forgot about that.'

I hadn't. Something about Dan had stayed with me. Dredged up memories, but of what I wasn't sure. Only that I knew him. He had an attractive face, but one you might forget, and an overall presence that didn't command you to notice him. His voice was a different thing altogether though. *That* I didn't think I'd forget. Which is what bothered me most. If I knew him at all, why wasn't I able to recall his voice from memory? Something felt wrong. Dan made my defences itch.

'Oh, well.' Aunt Lyrica shrugged. 'I'm not his PA, if anyone calls they can leave a message on the answerphone.'

When we got back to The Zoltan, there were no messages on the answerphone and no sign of Dan. I wondered if he was in his room watching television or reading a book. Or if he was still out taking photographs. I imagined he'd have captured plenty of greyscale seascapes. Each of them haunted by a summer long gone. Darkly seduced by waves crashing onto the jagged shore of Sandsend's stretch of winter-apocalypse beach. Gulls like white spectres would be suspended against a backdrop of violent sky. And the empty, broken shells and lone, dismembered pincers of crabs would mark the existential threat of death and eventual destruction of everything.

The more I thought about Dan, the more captivated I became. Perhaps obsessed would be a fairer word. But what was the hold he had over me? I didn't understand. And what was the uneasy nausea that stirred beneath the mild, yet indifferent, attraction I felt towards him? I certainly wasn't impulsive with men. Never had been. So what was it about Dan from Room Two that made me anxious but fascinated? Made my heart beat that little faster – mostly out of fear. I felt like I recognised him, yet I absolutely didn't.

Maybe, just maybe, I was trying to nurture a romantic notion, as hopeless as a dead rose in a bone-dry vase, that he was the Count to my Elisabeta. The rose's petals flakes of skin from my desiccated vampire.

I long. I long. I long.

Later that evening, in Aunt Lyrica's private lounge, she and I snuggled together beneath a red fleecy blanket and watched a documentary about women serial killers. We drank hot chocolate with shots of Irish cream liqueur for kicks, and now and then found ourselves entranced by the Christmas tree's chaser lights. I thought we'd make a cosy picture. One for the album, not the wall.

By ten o'clock it had been dark for well over five hours. A flurry of snow had come and gone since Aunt Lyrica and I were out with Kevin, but none of it had lain. I hadn't heard the rattle of the front door in all that time. Nor the creak of the stairs to the first floor. The entire guesthouse beyond the lounge loomed like a threatening presence. Breathing and watching. I'd never been so aware of it before.

'Dan must be back already,' I said.

Aunt Lyrica cocked one of her eyebrows. 'You seem very concerned about him, I must say.'

'Not concerned, just intrigued.' I shrugged, feigning a small amount of apathy. The television screen filled with the bespectacled face of Rose West looking like anyone's middle-aged neighbour; someone you'd expect to enjoy knitting blankets for the church raffle and reading Mills & Boon paperbacks on her floral Dralon couch.

Aunt Lyrica shifted in her seat, tucking her legs and feet beneath her. She looked like a cat. A luxuriating cat. 'Taken a shine to Dan the man, have we?'

'Not at all. I'm just being nosy.' I was more like a dog. A less flexible, sturdy-boned mongrel of indeterminable bloodline. 'If he's not back already, he might be stranded at Sandsend.'

'Or drinking at The Board Inn.'

'Or lying dead on the beach. How would we know?'

Aunt Lyrica made a face, not in the least bit fazed. 'I guess we won't till tomorrow when he doesn't show for breakfast. Then we can search for him and if we find him frozen to death on the beach, you can prise his Nikon from his stiff fingers and providing the battery's not flat have a look at his pictures. See what his last moments were. Beauty of digital, eh? Immediate gratification for an 'I want everything yesterday' kind of world. That'd sate your nosy cow disposition, wouldn't it?'

'Hmmm, possibly. What sort of stuff do you think he takes photos of?'

'How the hell should I know? I don't vet guests on their interests and endeavours. They're free to do whatever they like, as long as they leave their rooms as they find them and obey the 'no smoking' rule.' She unfurled one of her legs and nudged my thigh with her foot. 'But I suppose you can always give him a knock, see if he's in. Offer a turndown service.' She winked. 'I'm sure if you ask nicely he'll show you what he's got.'

'Don't be so vulgar.' I shoved her leg with my foot, but grinned. 'Do you reckon it's his job?'

'Photography?' She shrugged, looked fairly uninterested. 'Could be a hobby.'

'But in Whitby a week before Christmas on his own? *Really?*'

'What's wrong with that? You've no idea what his circumstances are. Besides, there are a billion worse things he could be doing. Like selling drugs to kids.'

'How do you know he doesn't?'

'The same way I don't know for sure he didn't garrotte a fisherman today and throw his body in the harbour.'

'Does he seem the sort who might?'

'Bloody hell, Cat, am I Mystic Meg suddenly? As long as he's not smoking up there, I don't care what he gets up to.'

'But aren't you a little curious about the people you have under your roof?'

Aunt Lyrica made wide eyes and gestured to the telly. More images of Rose West were showing. 'I find it pays not to be.' She handed her empty mug over. 'Now stop being such a busybody and go get your favourite aunt something with more alcohol. There's a bottle of Shiraz on the side. Or Chardonnay in the fridge. Surprise me.'

I didn't mention Dan any more. Decided I'd said enough, even though my thoughts kept returning to him. My subconscious was behaving neurotically, denying me access to something I sensed was just as dangerous as it was important. I wanted to know what and resolved to find out.

A couple of hours later, when I turned in for the night, I couldn't help but pause outside the door to Room Two. I wondered if Dan was inside. There were no sounds, but I had an inkling he was there. I could imagine his presence as a full heaviness pushing against the other side of the door. I let myself into my room and locked the door behind me, then pressed my ear against the adjoining wall. Dan's room buzzed with a thick silence. The same sort that filled my own.

Loneliness will sit over our roofs with brooding wings.
I had no doubt.

I unpacked my clothes, hanging some in the wardrobe and stashing the rest in the drawers by the door. I'd brought my laptop and black leather-bound work diary too, which I set out on top of the dresser by the window. Even though I'd been a virtual PA for five years, I never relied wholly on technology to keep my business and social affairs in order. Preferred to do it the old-fashioned way, with pen and paper. Being a homeworker meant I could take my work with me anywhere. There was no need for me to rush home. I hadn't decided how long I'd stay at The Zoltan. Hopefully, I thought, till my vampire was hydrated and healthy enough to do cartwheels down Crescent Avenue.

I took a white waffle spa-type robe from my case – couldn't remember where I'd got it, but was certain I hadn't bought it – then laid it out on the bed, pretending it was the vampire's withered body. As I stashed my empty suitcase under the bed, I already knew deep down I wouldn't need it for quite some time. The vampire had a lot of healing left to do.

7

Lyrica Black

2019

Lyrica switched the channel over and squinted at the television screen, trying to make out the faces of whoever was on the rerun of The Jonathan Ross Show. Gordon Ramsay was one guest, but his was the only name and face she could place. The wine she'd drunk had given her a dry mouth and the beginnings of a headache, but she pondered whether to have one more glass. It was just after eleven. Catherine had gone to bed. Usually Lyrica stayed up till at least midnight before going to her room to read for however much longer it took for sleep to arrive.

She'd had trouble with insomnia ever since Ged had passed away. And whenever she did manage to nod off, it was always with the bedside lamp on. She didn't like the dark. Couldn't bear to be in the same room as too many shadows. Knowing they were elsewhere in the building made her edgy, but she couldn't help that. The dark spaces other rooms kept were out of her control. It was impossible to have every room lit up all the time. Besides, if she went down that route, trying to assume utter control, where would it end? Because there were always other shadows somewhere close by – in wardrobes, under the floorboards, in the space behind the bath panel, in the house next door. You could drive yourself crazy just thinking about it.

The past week had seen Lyrica's night-time restlessness escalate. Death and loss brought with it much agitation and anxiety. Lyrica thought she should be used to it by now. Evidently not. She felt bad about not having gone to Jeanette's funeral, but the truth was she didn't want to have to say goodbye to her little sister because that would be to accept that she was no longer around. Which in turn highlighted her own failings. Because despite being married to a man who'd given her all she'd ever hoped for (love and a sense of security), Jeanette had succumbed to the monstrous vice she'd battled over the years. Drink. Not even Patrick had known the extent of her addiction, which made Lyrica realise she'd been wrong to assume her sister's marriage was much like her own. But Patrick Hill wasn't Ged Black. Ged had noticed every nuance of character in Lyrica. Even knew when she changed shampoo, because she smelt different. So just how wrong had she been in her evaluation of Jeanette and Patrick's marriage? It's easy to see what you want to see from the outside looking in. For the sake of your own peace of mind, especially. But what support did Jeanette really have? All of this reflection was too little, too late, of course. As her older sister, the one who knew Jeanette's demons better than anyone else, Lyrica thought she should have known her sister was having problems. Should have seen the signs, if only she'd looked harder. But Jeanette had kept the struggle entirely to herself. She'd kept Lyrica in the dark. And in the dark they'd both known bad things lurked.

As for Catherine, Lyrica thought her niece seemed to have taken things well. But who knew for certain? Catherine wasn't conventional in many respects. Hardly surprising, all things considered. Lyrica didn't expect Catherine to mourn Jeanette in any typical sense of a daughter having lost her mother. Theirs had been a difficult relationship.

It's like a disease growing inside me, Jeanette had told Lyrica during the early stages of her pregnancy. A malignant cancer, killing me.

It's a baby, Lyrica had said, issuing a small laugh and hoping Jeanette was being overly dramatic – hormonal, even. *Your* baby. Wait till it's born, you'll love it more than anything.

But Lyrica couldn't have been more wrong.

Kevin sat up in his basket by the radiator, his dark eyes twinkling. The Christmas tree's flickering lights made his wiry fur look alive with black flames. He issued a soft whine.

'Hey, Kev, what's up?' Lyrica said, relieved for the distraction from melancholic thoughts and the uselessness of hindsight. All the could haves, should haves and would haves which painted the past in harsh tones of regret. 'Do you need to go in the yard?'

This question prompted Kevin to stand. He gave his body a shake in preparation, then his claws *rick-ticked* on the floor as he trotted over.

Lyrica pushed herself off the couch. 'Come on then, buggerlugs.' She led him to the lounge door, and when she pulled it open, a thick wall of black startled her.

Catherine must have turned all the lights off.

But why?

Does it matter? Just turn them back on.

Lyrica bit her lip. Didn't make any attempt to move. The switch for the hall light was near the front door; an impossibly long way off with so much darkness and any amount of hidden depths in between. A sharp burst of laughter from the television mangled her nerves. It sounded insincere, perhaps even directed at her.

You gonna stand there all night? Kevin looked up at her expectantly, head cocked to one side, waiting for her to do something. She took a deep breath. Faint streetlight seeped in through the bevelled glass of the front door, creating an orangey rectangle that looked melted to the wall. She focussed on that as she edged down the hall.

A loaded quiet, offset by intermittent eruptions from the television, filled the core of the building with a sombre heaviness. As though The Zoltan was holding its breath, dreading what might unfurl from its own darkness. Lyrica fingered the wooden spindles of the balustrade as she passed the stairs. There was a swishing noise halfway up. Fabric crinkling. She snatched her hand back and clutched it to her chest. 'Cat?'

There was no answer. No further movement.

When she drew level with the dining room on her right, there came a muted but distinct sound of hissing from behind the closed door. Lyrica came over all woozy, couldn't imagine ever escaping this dark dread if she was to look. But she had to see inside. Had to check if whether, unbidden, the snakes had breached their plaster confines. She reached out, pushed open the door and peered inside.

A darkness just as hostile as that in the hall lay within, and the hissing was almost deafening. Not only that, she could also make out the *click-click-clicking* of hundreds of beetle legs and wings inside the walls, a plague of unwanted pests encapsulating the entire room. She imagined a nest of serpentine bodies twisting and twining at the bottom of the fireplace, spilling out and covering the entire carpet, exploring and wrapping themselves around furniture legs. Forked tongues licking the air. She stifled a whimper and searched for the light switch with her trembling hand. Expected her fingers to brush against some kind of insect-grotesque; hard exoskeletons, antennae, scores of many jointed legs. Quick and nimble. Straight up her arm. Inside her clothes.

Mary had a little lamb. Mary had a little lamb. Mary had a little lamb.

Her fingers touched wallpaper. Then the plastic light switch. When the light flashed on, the hissing stopped.

Abrupt silence buzzed in Lyrica's ears, fizzling into her thoughts but not enough to smother them. And the tidiness of the dining room taunted her. There was nothing out of place. Yet with the visually loud starkness of familiarity, she realised nothing was right either. The entire room was like a staged scene of supposed banality. If she so much as closed her eyes, everything would rearrange and she'd be someplace else – till she opened her eyes again. Something squirmed on the canvas on the chimneybreast; a worm on the stalk of the crimson rose's black shadow. But when she looked closer, there was nothing but paint. A trick of the light.

All of it a trick.

You're being ridiculous.

Lyrica knocked the light switch down, feeling annoyed and immersing herself in blackness. She closed the door behind her and waited. Listened for the snakes to return. When they didn't, she continued along the hall.

Almost there.

She passed the bottom of the stairs and the same shush-shushing of fabric she'd heard before made her freeze. This time she saw movement from the corner of her eye. A black shape about halfway up the stairs. An adult figure, crouching. Watching. Lurking. When she turned her head fully, there was no one there.

'Cat?' she called, her tremulous voice too thin to find its way far the gloom. 'Is it you? Are you up?'

There was no reply.

Lyrica backed away from the stairway, too afraid to turn her back to it. Too afraid of the shapes that might manifest and bloom behind her eyes, projecting themselves onto the surrounding darkness, thus making the dark and herself unreliable.

What was real and what wasn't?

There was a swooshing movement of air behind her, then something hard and thin struck the back of her calves. White, splintering pain exploded behind her eyes. She fell forward, collapsing to her hands and knees. There was another shifting of air and Lyrica squeezed her eyes shut, expecting another agonising blow. None came. She swivelled onto her backside, so she was sitting upright with her legs sprawled in front, then scrabbled backwards. A black figure loomed over her. Substantial. Defined. No retinal trickery.

'You ran off and left her,' Sister Gregory said, her voice a near-death experience revisited. Lyrica's insides twisted and contracted. Even now, in Lyrica's adulthood, the old nun was a formidable figure, her tallness and broadness perhaps emphasised by the voluminous folds of the habit she wore. Her face was a hideous grey death mask, from under which beetles scurried through the eye and mouth holes. And that mouth. Oh God, that mouth. It was impossibly wide and spewed forth the reek of rotting flesh, freeing too many memories Lyrica had suppressed for her own good.

'No.' Lyrica shook her head, cowering low.

'Yes, you did.' Sister Gregory reached out and seized Lyrica by the upper arm, her corpse fingers gripping too tight, digging into tender flesh. 'Running away is what you're good at, you Hall women.'

Lyrica felt her throat closing, such was her fear. She tried to suck in air, but it wouldn't go down. Her lungs were too frantic. Heartbeat frenzied.

'Poor little Jeanette died all alone,' the old nun crooned, revelling in the fear she still inspired. She flexed her grip, squeezing even tighter.

Lyrica yelped. 'No, she didn't. Patrick was there.'

'Do you know that for certain?' When Lyrica didn't respond, Sister Gregory laughed. 'Of course you don't. It's not like you were ever there for her.'

'I was always there for her.'

'Not when it mattered. You escaped from Eden House

and left her there.'

'I never escaped.'

'Jeanette would say differently. You could have done more.'

'I tried my best.'

'It wasn't good enough.'

'Shut up!' Rage swelled in Lyrica's chest; a dangerous surge of self-hate and frustration. Red dots danced behind her eyes.

'Misfortune follows you round like a destructive dog that you can't tame or get rid of.' Sister Gregory shuddered with muted laughter. Gravel crunched in her chest. 'Your parents died because you and your sister were unbearable brats. Your husband died because he couldn't keep up with you. Your daughter left because she couldn't stand you. And your sister died because you were too self-absorbed to see the truth.'

Lyrica's lips pulled back in a snarl, but she had no words with which to respond.

'The truth was always there for you to see,' Sister Gregory said. 'So obvious, if you'd only wanted to see it.'

'You're a liar.' Lyrica tried to shake herself loose, imagined bruises already blooming beneath the nun's fingers. Pockets of blood collecting under her skin from crushed blood vessels. 'You always were.'

'I suppose I'm not being wholly fair,' Sister Gregory said, maintaining her grip. 'Tom Dockin ate your eyes years ago. You've been blind to everything ever since.'

'Tom Dockin's not real.'

'You know that's not true. He spent quite some time relishing the taste of your heart too. There's a hole where it used to be. It's filled with bile. Does it still hurt? I bet it does. I bet the memory of a full, contented heart makes you want to die.'

'Shut up.'

'Your soul will be next.'

'What about your soul?' Lyrica hissed. 'Did Tom Dockin eat that? *Did he?*'

Sister Gregory's mouth stretched wider and a snake's glistening head appeared where her tongue should be. Its eyes were deep red, the colour of old blood, hypnotically incandescent and obscene and impossible in the darkness. Lyrica saw its black forked tongue tasting the air and watched in horror as its thick body began to ascend from the stinking depths of the old nun's guts. She held her breath. Tried to shuffle away as it bridged the gap, sliding towards her. But Sister Gregory held onto her arm, keeping her in place. Immobile.

When the snake reached the base of Lyrica's throat, she didn't dare swallow. Hardly dared to breathe. It began to coil around her neck, its muscular body winding tighter and tighter, slick with Sister Gregory's saliva. She tried to reach up, to prise it away, but Sister Gregory grabbed her wrists and held them fast.

'If you hadn't run away,' Sister Gregory said, once the snake was fully disgorged from her mouth, 'Jeanette might not have had that badness sown in her.' She laughed, a rough hacking noise which sounded more like choking. And maybe it was the sound of choking, Lyrica thought. Only that of her own, because the snake kept applying more pressure to her neck. Harsher and firmer, till the darkness was tinged with red. All the blood pounding in her head, behind her eyes.

Mary had a little lamb.

'Did Jeanette ever tell you who fathered that bastard upstairs?' Sister Gregory said, leaning closer. Her breath was a humid blast of the worst decay imaginable.

Lyrica closed her eyes.

Its fleece was white as snow.

'She never did, did she?' Sister Gregory taunted. 'When Jeanette refused to tell you, you left it at that. You could have insisted, but you didn't. You were too busy getting on with your life, your own pregnancy, to risk rocking the boat. Were you relieved she didn't tell you? Of course you were. Not knowing was less responsibility for you, wasn't it?'

Lyrica felt something crunch. Heard something snap.

Windpipe or vertebrae?

Sister Gregory cackled.

Lyrica fell backwards and a true black with no variation of any other shade filled all the spaces inside her head, drowning her eyes, killing her senses. When she could see again, nothing made sense. She was lying on the couch, and the telly was tuned in to some late night gambling show. 'And what a great night we're having,' said the orange-faced host.

Lyrica lurched upright, her hands clutching her throat.

There was no snake.

It was just a nightmare.

Kevin whined. He looked at her from his basket, his eyes keen, his fur dancing in fairy light flashes. It was too much like déjà vu. Lyrica sat up and eyed the door. Would Sister Gregory be waiting in the hallway with the red-eyed snake? Kevin trotted over, as if prompting her to find out. She stood up and crept to the door, listening all the while for sounds beyond the lounge. There were none. She counted to five, then snatched open the door. She sagged with relief when the welcome glow of the hallway light flushed over her. Warm and familiar and safe.

'Come on,' she said to Kevin, managing a weary smile. 'Let's go.' But as she led the way to the rear of the house, her pyjama bottoms brushed against the back of her legs, making her aware of a stinging sensation. A new dread bubbled up inside. Made her thoughts scream with heightening hysteria. She bent and hitched up both hems to look, and found the fresh and inflamed thin vertical welts of Mr Birchwood across each calf.

8

Catherine Hall

2019

The duck down duvet crackled every time I moved. I imagined it was the vampire's crepe paper skin. The idea was somewhat soothing. That I had something to tend to, to nurse back to health – even if it was my own mental state – gave me purpose. Something to focus on. Reaching out, I patted the sleeve of the waffle dressing gown and laughed; an inward sort of giggle, within which I noted a disturbed sense of madness. Aunt Lyrica's supply of wine had gone to my head.

I am all in a sea of wonders. I doubt; I fear; I think strange things, which I dare not confess to my own soul.

My breath caught in my throat.

Was there something I needed to confess?

A grey area where ideas of Dan, a possible past acquaintance and many other uncertainties roiled in my mind. Buried beneath many layers of distinct memories, this grey area, dark and dangerous, remained unreachable. Inaccessible. But was this lack of detail down to disinterest, like when you put something unimportant away and can't find it again? Or something more troubling, like self-preservation? Because I must admit, a feeling beyond my usual contentment to be back at The Zoltan troubled me greatly. Something as unpleasant as an insect bite that's impossible to ignore and needs to be scratched, even though you know it'll make things worse, had got under my skin. Suddenly the guesthouse didn't seem as inviting as it had when I'd first arrived. Empty rooms elsewhere in the building felt full with… vague animosity? That they might hoard more darkness than any other night made me nervous.

It was then that Aunt Lyrica's words came back to me: *I think she's here.*

Calanthe.

Could the suggestion of my cousin's spirit at The Zoltan have spooked me? Or was I feeling whatever Aunt Lyrica could?

I don't know what to do, Aunt Lyrica had said. *Just listen for her, Cat. See if she'll talk to you.*

'Calanthe?' The shadows in the room seemed to reverberate in thick, silent response. 'Are you here?'

A gust of wind rattled the window sill. I jumped in alarm. Whatever was taking shape in all the unseen places in The Zoltan, it was threatening. The room next door, in particular, pulsed with hidden blackness. A loud heartbeat against my wall. I feared the *thump-thump-thump* of Dan's presence would give me fevered dreams. And all I could think was: he's come for me! The words so defined, so credible in my mind, I had no doubt they had true meaning. But how to decipher that meaning?

Was Dan part of the growing darkness?

Or was the darkness a consequence of my own fear?

The vampire's fingers slotted around mine like warm chrysalises filled with ruin or salvation, and I drifted to sleep listening to Dan's beating heart and the shushing sounds of the North Sea as I thought them to be on such a cold, wintry night.

My subconscious delivered me to a dining room I'd never dined in before. A great hall, in fact. Much grander than the one I'd always imagined inside myself. It must have been impressive at one time, but was not much more than museum chic now – everything dusty and dated. Long, curtainless windows ran along the length of the room on both sides, ten in total. They were gaping black voids, allowing the voyeuristic night to become part of the room. I was sitting at one end of a long mahogany table, separated by a vast polished expanse from my mother, Uncle Ged and Calanthe, who were all seated at the other end. I was the invisible cat and there was the ghost of a beautiful blonde girl and a snake-entwined skull. All the room was missing was the velvety witch to make it (me) complete. Evidently my mother was a substitute for the velvety witch, which was no substitute at all. I glowered at her.

Each of us had a silver goblet in front of us. I couldn't see what was in the others, they were too far away, but dark red liquid filled mine. Wine or blood, it was hard to say. Sensibly it would be wine, but when are dreams ever sensible? I lifted the goblet and sniffed. The liquid had an earthy smell, not unlike an animal. I imagined it would be too warm and sit heavy in my stomach, so I put the goblet back down without drinking from it.

Calanthe raised hers and toasted the air. 'My dearest Wilhelmina,' she said, in a theatrical tone that was so very Calanthe. Her wide blue eyes suggested a gentle innocence which her full-lipped smirk contradicted. 'That thing you did… well, it was the most impressive thing you ever did. I mean…' She laid her left hand flat on her chest for added effect. 'Colour me shocked to absolute fuck.'

Uncle Ged shifted in his seat and coughed into his hand. 'Language, sweetheart.'

Calanthe laughed, the sound light and appealing, like a finch's chirrup but with dark undertones of malice. 'Oh, Dad, don't be such a prude.' Then to me, she said, 'Didn't know you had it in you, my otherwise unimaginative, dull-witted cousin. Touché.' She took a sip from her goblet and when she withdrew it, her top lip was too opaquely red for the contents to be wine. Keeping her eyes on mine, she slid her tongue out and lapped up the residue; a slow, tantalising effort. Almost seductive in nature. Again, Calanthe all over. The world's biggest actress. Centre of attention.

'You ruined everything,' my mother announced, her attention on me. Cold and blank, her eyes conveyed a level of hostility she'd never revealed in life. She didn't raise her glass in a toast. Not even to congratulate me on destroying her life. A pretty big achievement by anyone's standards, surely.

'Now come on, Jeanie,' Uncle Ged objected. His fingers twitched and, in what seemed like an indecisive impulse, an uncomfortable obligation to soothe her, he patted the back of my mother's left hand. 'That's a bit harsh, isn't it?'

'Not at all.' My mother didn't move. Didn't even blink. 'It's the truth.'

Uncle Ged sat back in his chair and puffed out his cheeks. When nobody said anything else, he threw me a wink and said, 'Well, I love you, baby girl.'

Calanthe gasped. 'You know what she did though, right?'

'Oh, you girls.' Uncle Ged rolled his eyes and wafted a hand in the air. 'Stop telling tales.'

'But there's one tale that won't stop telling itself, isn't there, Gerard?' my mother said with mounting tension. Tendons stood out on her scrawny neck, I didn't think she could look any more rigid. 'What do you propose we do about *that*?'

Uncle Ged ran a hand over his face and groaned. 'Christ, Jeanie. Not this again.'

A flash of white lightning lit up the windows, capturing each dining room guest as a split-second still. The light dazzled me, burning onto the back of my retinas. Beyond the window immediately to my right I saw the silhouette of a hulking great figure. Tall and broad. Long black coat.

No one else seemed to notice.

Thunder boomed, shaking the entire table. Everyone looked up, as if the storm might present itself as an actual being who would levitate above us.

'He's here now,' my mother announced.

The space above the table remained empty, except for the dust-encrusted crystal chandelier which hung over us like an outdated epiphany that no longer made sense. Uncle Ged looked agitated and glanced around the room. 'Where? I don't see him.'

I looked to the window on my right. The figure had gone.

My mother closed her eyes, as if communing with the dead. 'You might not see him, but he's definitely here.'

'Oh yes,' Calanthe agreed, her pale face a serene Victorian death mask of macabre beauty. She looked at me as she spoke, her fiery blue eyes burning into mine. 'He's in our passions and desires; the juicy meat of our hearts. He's in everything we bear witness to; with our own eyes and the eyes of our demons. He's in our souls; our jet black souls. And he's in all of our lies; the debts to the truth which we choose to withhold. He's in all of those places, and what all of us are, what all of us contain, makes him grow stronger.'

'And he's ravenously hungry,' my mother said. 'Always hungry.'

Calanthe snapped her teeth together, creating a nauseating sound that made everything in the room shiver. 'And when he eats you up, Wilhelmina, which he will...' Her voice was now a viscous monotone, lacking its usual singsong drama. 'You'll make him fat. Disgustingly fat.'

I awoke with a start.

Darkness saturated the room and a rhythmic rocking sound vanquished fragments of the dream. I sat up.

Remembered where I was, but knew something wasn't right. There was a cloying odour of animal. The hot musk of a horse or goat. And mattress springs groaned somewhere close by. A woman moaned in a paroxysm of lust, before a man's voice, distant, yet right there in the room with me, said, 'I love your body… Your skin… You'd look good on my walls… Come with me.'

There was movement in the shadows. A mass of blackness more defined than the night's dark. A figure at the foot of the bed. Watching me. A man. A huge one at that. Then a new noise emanated from this terrifying presence. A metallic *snip snip snip*. My hand flew to my mouth as part of the past came screeching back to me with all the horror of a terminal illness.

He's come for me!

With this realisation, the man issued a low chortle that belched from his mouth like horse breath. The sound taunted every hair follicle on my body. My heart crashed against my breastbone.

My heart!

He's in our passions and desires; the juicy meat of our hearts.

I know you! I know who you are, I thought.

Scrabbling backwards, I pressed myself against the headboard. Pulled my knees to my chest. The vampire tried to get up too, to drag itself away. But it couldn't. Gasping for breath, it buried its face in the bedsheets and chanted: it can't be, it can't be, it can't be.

The air felt too hefty, like it might contain any amount of things that might touch me, and if anything should, I thought I might die.

'What do you want?' I asked, surprised I could talk.

When the man in the shadows who was much more than the shadows didn't reply, I flung my arm out and flicked the switch on the bedside lamp.

Nothing happened. The room remained lost to darkness.

Oh no Oh no Oh no!

I watched, barely able to breathe, as the man's obsidian silhouette moved closer. I could hear his feet brushing against the carpet, but the mental image my subconscious summoned was that of cloven hooves.

He's in everything we witness; with our own eyes and the eyes of our demons.

The closer he came, the louder the *snip snip snip* of metal skimming against metal became. It consumed my head; a horribly familiar sound, not as lost to me as whatever memories I had of Dan. I thought I might faint.

He's in our souls; our jet black souls.

My heart just about stopped when a peal of rapturous laughter filled the room. A laugh I hadn't heard in over sixteen years.

'Calanthe?' My voice was so ragged, I barely recognised it as my own.

He's in all of our lies; the debts to the truth which we choose to withhold.

The vampire's breathing was frantic beside me. It sounded as though it was being throttled.

Then I realised its ragged breaths were mine.

He's in all of those places and what all of us are, what all of us contain, makes him grow stronger.

I bolted from the bed, my frenzied hands searching the wall for the light switch.

He's ravenously hungry. Always hungry.

Light filled the room, and I saw there was no one else there with me. I was alone in Room One with all of its red accessories and the shrivelled vampire and the memory of a monster from many years ago.

My monster?

I have crossed oceans of time to find you.

No. Not mine. My mother's.

All those years ago she'd tainted my mind with her brokenness, yet somehow I'd forgotten all about Tom

Dockin. Till now. The bogeyman – or the Devil himself? – had caught up with me. And so too would everything else, I thought.

He'll make you scream, make you cry.

The vampire withered and cringed. I sat on the edge of the bed, unable to stop trembling. Unable to take my eyes away from the spot where Tom Dockin had stood. Unable to get the sound of Calanthe's laugh out of my head. I was afraid to be in any way compos mentis because reality was too scary. But then, what was real and what was fantasy? How could I know if I was sane? Lines had been crossed. Boundaries blurred.

And it all linked back to the day of Uncle Ged's funeral.

9

Catherine Hall

1997

The opening to Guns 'N' Roses' *November Rain* played from unseen speakers, filling the crematorium with a side to Ged Black that was more wistful than rock 'n' roll. An apt choice made by Aunt Lyrica. My mother was sitting to my right, Calanthe to my left. We were in the front row, along with Aunt Lyrica; VIPs at Uncle Ged's send off.

Calanthe was facing front, her eyes fixed on the coffin. She was as still as a statue, her blonde hair pulled away from her face. Secured at the back of her head with a black satin bow, it hung down to her waist in a thick, glossy mane ending in ringlets. All of it natural. Puffy pink eyelids spoiled her blue, baby-doll eyes, but she still looked pretty. A miniature version of Aunt Lyrica.

My hair was similarly pulled back, only mine was shorter and finer. Straggly to a point. A touch too brown to be considered proper blonde. Too straight for curls to form with any real definition, but too kinked to lie flat. My hair has always kept an awkward, wavy texture; forever windswept, needing to be brushed.

'I'm the same as you now,' Calanthe said, digging her knuckles into my thigh. We were sitting so close I could feel the warmth of her body. In total contrast, her countenance was cold.

'How do you mean?'

'I don't have a dad either.'

I considered this for a moment. Decided that our circumstances were not similar at all. She'd had Uncle Ged's love and guidance for ten years, and ten years was better than none. My situation was nowhere near as dramatic, in that I'd never lost what I'd never had. Not that it wasn't without its own hang-ups and long-lingering upsets.

'At least you know who he was,' I said.

'Shhh.' My mother elbowed me – a sharp, swift knock to the arm. She flashed a warning glare, her eyes crusty with cheap mascara and her lips pinched tight. She looked unhinged. Possibly high. Like some down-and-out on The Jerry Springer Show. Her hair was scraped back in a messy ponytail. I suspect she'd brushed it with her fingers, not a comb. She was a true blonde, same as Aunt Lyrica. They looked very similar, but not. My mother had the potential to be just as pretty, but a permanently haunted expression made her never so. She was too dark and lacklustre about the eyes. Appeared a little grey-skinned and emaciated. Even though it was Aunt Lyrica who was in mourning, it was my mother who looked the most afflicted. She always did. Like she was bereft of the entire world. I considered us – me and her – subpar versions of Aunt Lyrica and Calanthe.

At the behest of my mother's angry eyes, I faced front and watched as long velvet curtains drew together on an automatic track. Slowly they blocked Uncle Ged's coffin from sight, like a magician's prop. They were luxurious red, the sort you'd expect to see at the theatre or lining the cape of any Hollywood Dracula. I imagined Uncle Ged's coffin was on a conveyor belt and as soon as the curtains were fully closed, doors to a large fiery oven would open and the coffin would roll inside to be consumed by flames.

I wasn't sure what would happen afterwards, like how

soon Aunt Lyrica could collect his ashes, or what would happen once she did. Would she keep them in a silver urn on the mantelpiece at The Zoltan? Scatter them to the wind on the West Cliff? Or bury them at the cemetery? These were all possibilities, but I didn't think it was right for me to ask. Not today. I was certain my mother would know the answer, but didn't think I should bother her about it either. She seemed especially distant. Most of the time she had little to feed back to me except impatience.

Once the curtains had drawn and the formally dressed woman who'd conducted the service at the front of the room had given some final parting words, none of which I can remember, *November Rain* started up again, playing from speakers I hadn't identified. I'd seen the music video for *November Rain* on MTV many times. Loved the bit where Slash stands on the black piano Axl Rose is playing, while smoking a cigarette and playing his guitar and looking about as cool as anyone can. As everyone filed out of the crematorium, I pretended I was an extra in that music video, telling myself that if I turned round Slash would be there and none of this would be happening. Not really. It would all just be make-believe. So I didn't look back, didn't shatter the illusion.

My mother shuffled along next to me, behind Aunt Lyrica and Calanthe. Aunt Lyrica draped her arm across Calanthe's shoulders, squeezing her tight. Perfect mother. She looked gorgeous; dyed red hair twisted into an immaculate French pleat and a black lace veil partially covering her face. She was more glamorous than anyone I'd ever known.

When we reached the double doors at the rear of the building, which were propped open by solid stone doorstops in the shape of voluminously maned lions, I stepped into the grey day and was swallowed by a black crowd of mourners. Mostly they were Uncle Ged's biker mates, all of whom would have been wearing black anyway. Some ignored me, probably too immersed in their own grief to notice a plain waif in their midst, but others smiled sadly or winked affectionately to acknowledge my loss. Their loss. Our shared loss.

Aunt Lyrica announced she'd made sandwiches and pastries back at The Zoltan and invited everyone back. Calanthe had told me earlier this would happen, she'd said it was called a wake. I could tell my mother wanted to decline the invitation, but it would have been rude of her not to go. Uncaring, even. So after a hasty cigarette outside the crematorium with a woman called Pat who wore a cheap nylon blouse and old lady perfume, my mother ushered me to the car and we travelled, just the two of us, to The Zoltan. She barely spoke to me on the way, biting the skin around her fingernails a lot.

When we got to Crescent Avenue all the spaces near The Zoltan had been taken, so my mother parked at the other end of the street, outside a B&B which looked like it was still rooted in the eighties. I got out of the car and, without waiting for her, ran to The Zoltan; the place I wished was my home.

In the hallway, I found dozens of people standing about in small clusters already, their sombre chatter creating an almost maddening buzz. Cigarette smoke gathered above everyone's heads like building blueish rain clouds. I spotted Calanthe on the stairs, halfway up. She was sitting with her elbows resting on her knees, fist propping her chin.

I pushed my way past an overweight man with a shaved head and tattooed face, almost knocking a cup of tea from his hands. 'Watch how you go, love,' a woman with frizzy black hair said, grabbing my shoulder to slow me. I ignored her and scampered up the stairs, then sat on the one beneath Calanthe.

'How long do you think they'll stay?' Calanthe said, glaring at the mourners below.

'Dunno.' I'd never been to a wake before. Didn't know what was supposed to happen, never mind what etiquette existed for such gatherings.

'I want them all to go away. For them to stop eating our food and to just leave us be.' Calanthe's scowl was fierce, but it quickly relaxed into a defeated frown. 'But I also don't want them to go. Because when they do, it'll be quiet. And there are too many rooms to be filled with all that quiet. It'll be horrible, like when you bite a wool sleeve and there's that awful squeak you can't hear, but you can feel it against your teeth all the same. And it'll be there all the time. Can you imagine?'

I could. As disarrayed as The Zoltan currently was, there was something comforting about the noise and bustle of adults that filled the downstairs rooms. It was a distraction from what had happened. It was easy to pretend that Uncle Ged might be down there now, amongst the crowd; his cigarette smoke adding to the ghostly haze, his gruff voice adding to the general hubbub. But when everyone was to leave and go home, I didn't dare imagine just how awful the subsequent silence would be. How loudly our memories would call to us.

My mother appeared in the hallway, slipping in through the front door like a tormented spirit. No one seemed to notice, except me and Calanthe. She looked out of place, like she didn't belong.

'Is Aunt Jeanette back on the booze?' Calanthe asked.

I shrugged. My mother looked tired and overly thin, but I didn't know if either of those things was a sign she was drinking excessive (or any) amounts of alcohol. I didn't even know how much alcohol was considered too much. Calanthe had told me many times that my mother was a recovering alcoholic, but I didn't understand what that meant. Not really. And I was too embarrassed to ask.

'She doesn't look too good,' Calanthe insisted.

'She looks the same as she always does,' I said,

disinterested.

'She's dead skinny. Would probably snap if there's a strong wind.' Calanthe stood up and nudged past me with her foot, making her way downstairs. 'Maybe she'll die next.'

'Hmmm.' Maybe. I got up and followed. Couldn't help but think I wouldn't mind if she was to die, because then I might get to live at The Zoltan permanently and Aunt Lyrica would adopt me.

I trailed behind Calanthe like her shadow as we mingled with Uncle Ged's friends. They all adored her, and I found it hard not to be jealous. Couldn't think of any situation where I'd receive similar attention.

Giant, hairy bikers who'd drunk tea from delicate china cups soon swigged beer straight from cans. I wondered at what point they'd identify as alcoholics, because it was only late afternoon and that didn't seem like an appropriate time for drinking. I kept a careful eye on my mother, to see what she was drinking. She stuck close to Aunt Lyrica and whatever was in the Tony the Tiger mug she drank from remained a mystery.

When Calanthe got bored with the adults' reminiscing, she ordered me to her room to do some 'fashion designing' in her sketchbook. This involved her sketching and me watching. I was supposed to be in awe of her talents. And I suppose I was. She had a flare for drawing and a knack for designing wonderful outfits, most of them Victorian-inspired but ultra modern. She said she wanted to be a fashion designer one day. I've no doubt if she hadn't disappeared she'd have been up there with the likes of Vivien Westwood.

Much later, when we emerged, both of us were hungry. Everyone had cleared off, except my mother. We heard her and Aunt Lyrica's voices in the lounge, and the sound of Aunt Lyrica crying. Calanthe put a finger to her lips and, together, we crept along the hall till we reached the lounge door. I expected the lounge would be littered with empty teacups and beer cans, but when we poked our heads inside this wasn't the case at all. The room had been completely tidied. What surprised me more, however, was that Aunt Lyrica had removed her veil and appeared composed, if a little weary, and it was *she* who was consoling my mother.

What on earth did my mother have to be so upset about?

'I think you should see a counsellor,' Aunt Lyrica said. She stood up from the couch and put her hands on her hips, then paced back and forth on the strip of carpet in front of the couch, like a cat in stockinged feet.

Calanthe turned to me, her eyes wide, and pressed a finger to her lips again. Not that I needed a prompt to stay quiet.

'What's the point?' my mother said, her face ugly and blotchy from sobbing. She dabbed at her cheeks with a paper handkerchief.

'Because you need help.'

'And how's a counsellor going to help me?'

'Because I think you have Post Traumatic Stress Disorder, and they deal with this stuff. It's what they do.'

My mother wafted a hand in the air to reject Aunt Lyrica's diagnosis. She wiped her nose with the scrunched up tissue and shook her head. 'It's got nothing to do with stress, I've seen him too many times.'

I didn't know much of anything about stress, but in that moment my mother looked vulnerable. Afraid, even.

'It's not possible.' Aunt Lyrica kept striding back and forth, worrying her bottom lip with her fingers and deep in thought. It was the most troubled I'd ever seen her. 'I think we should seek legal advice.'

'Legal advice?' My mother made a high-pitched, hysterical sound. A strangulated laugh, perhaps. 'What would that achieve?'

'I dunno.' Aunt Lyrica stopped marching. 'Some sort of

justice might make you feel better. If you'd just talk…
Open up… Talk to *me* about it.'

'Nothing will make me feel better. That place, it never leaves me.'

'I know, but if you'd only just…'

My mother issued a harrowing groan from the depths of whatever despair she had bottled within, a truly frightening sound, then she cried freely.

Aunt Lyrica rushed to the couch and bundled her into a hug. 'Hey now, hush. I'm here.' She rocked my mother back and forth in her arms. 'Nothing's going to hurt you. It'll be okay.'

They remained in that embrace for a while, till eventually my mother said in an eerily flat voice, 'I'm sorry, I shouldn't be putting all of this on you. Not today. Especially not today. I should have gone home and taken Catherine with me. Left you to grieve in peace.'

'Don't be ridiculous.' Aunt Lyrica swept a strand of wayward hair from my mother's face, tucking it behind her ear. 'There's no peace to be had in grief, and you damn well know that. Besides, you're my little sister, you can come to me any time you like. No matter what. I want you here tonight. Cat too. She's good for Calanthe. The three of you, you're all the family I have.'

My mother seemed to consider this, then nodded.

'He can't hurt you, you know.' Aunt Lyrica said, rubbing the back of my mother's hand.

My mother seemed suddenly prickly. 'Can't he?'

'No.'

'I wish I could believe that, but I can't. He's with me all the time. I see him when I'm sleeping. And when I'm awake. I see him every time…' She closed her eyes and buried her face in her hands.

'Every time what?'

'I look at her.'

Who?

Calanthe tugged on my sleeve and mouthed, *She means you.*

Could it be true?

It certainly seemed plausible, because who else might she be talking about?

Perplexed, I mouthed back, *But who's he?*

Calanthe rolled her eyes as if to say *Come on, dummy, keep up.* 'Your dad,' she whispered.

I shook my head. Felt chilled to my core.

Could it really be?

'You're a survivor,' Aunt Lyrica said to my mother. 'And she's a massive positive to be taken from all the negative you harbour. If you'd only see it that way, you'd win.'

But my mother looked anything but convinced. In fact, she seemed to retreat further into herself, to whatever madness tormented her.

Calanthe dragged me to the kitchen, our eavesdropping over. Part of me wished I'd heard none of what we'd heard. If I was a huge positive to be taken from something so negative, what exactly had my mother survived? The truth had been hinted at, left to take shape in the innocence of my mind. But did I truly want to know the full extent?

He's with me all the time. I see him when I'm sleeping. I see him when I'm awake. I see him every time… I look at her.

I couldn't help but wonder if next time I looked in the mirror, I'd see my father staring back.

We made fish finger sandwiches, not talking much at all. Then later that night, when I was lying in Calanthe's bed, restless and anxious, I made shapes out of the shadows in the corner where the wardrobe was. It had been a long, exhausting day, but too many negative thoughts rolled and churned in my mind, offering no clear resolution. They promised only long-term confusion, self-doubt and sadness.

'Do you think my dad was a bad person?' I said to Calanthe, unable to refrain any longer from seeking her opinion. I wanted her to say no. Then to tell me in her best storytelling manner that there must be some tragic, romantic story of my origin. Like perhaps my father had died in a terrible accident and my mother was too sad to regale stories of him. But she didn't. After a few moments of silence, she said, 'He must have been an absolute monster.'

'A *monster?*' I hadn't expected that.

'Why else would he be a secret?' Calanthe shifted onto her side, her warm breath unpleasant on my face, her knees pressed against my leg, digging in. 'It's probably best if you don't know about him.'

Both of us fell quiet after that, my head filled with all kinds of monsters. Sleep wouldn't come easily that night, I knew, and I was still awake some time later when a strange metallic grating noise started up somewhere out in the hallway. Not exactly loud, but enough to draw attention. The underside of my face prickled with newfound dread. In all the times I'd stayed at The Zoltan, it wasn't a sound I was familiar with. There was something deliberate and menacing about the repetitive rhythm. Something that pulled on my instincts; a darkness, a threat, a warning that something was about to happen that I'd do well to ignore.

'Calanthe?' I said, encircling her wrist with my fingers. 'Are you awake?'

'Yes.'

'What's that noise?'

'I don't know.'

I'd hoped with all of my being that she would. And because she didn't, the room seemed suddenly darker. Shadows grew bigger and deeper as though they had a life of their own and might form a collective mouth and swallow the bed whole.

Calanthe shook free from my grasp, slipping out of bed and heading to the door. I wanted to cry out, to beg her to come back, because I didn't want to be alone, not in this overbearing darkness, but I didn't. Instead, I launched out of bed and stumbled after her, groping for her lithe body. When I found it, I clutched her waist, not caring that my fingers pinched too tightly. At the insistence of the strange sound beyond the room, I scrabbled along behind her. I wasn't sure why the darkness troubled me so much, but it did. Badness filled every shadow. There was an oppressive air of death in the house, weighing down on us. Not the heart-breaking aftermath of Uncle Ged's passing but a brand new threat.

Calanthe inched open the door. I peered over her shoulder into the long, dark hallway. As if alerted to our prying, the noise stopped. My ears filled with the ensuing silence, packing my skull with building tension. Then a skeletal figure flitted along the passageway, zagging out of view into the lounge.

My mother.

My initial thought was that she must be sleepwalking, or wandering about in a drunken stupor, if that's what alcoholics do, unable to sleep. From inside the lounge she began to whisper; a frantic, incessant chant that made the hairs on my arms stand upright. Trepidation clawed up from my gut, coating the back of my throat with the sourness of bile. I swallowed it back down, but it rose again just as quickly. Something bad was about to happen. I knew.

Calanthe must have thought so too. Her body was tense as she began to tiptoe down the hall. I kept some of the fabric of her nightgown bunched in both of my fists. I wasn't keen to go anywhere near the lounge, but had little choice but to follow or else I'd be left alone in the hissing, scratchy darkness. I tried to convince myself that my imagination had created way more terror than light would have allowed, but deep down, intuitively, I sensed danger. Though whether a broken mind or an otherworldly connection, I didn't know.

Is there a difference between them?

I'm still not sure.

When we reached the lounge, my mother was huddled on the floor in the darkness; a thorny silhouette on her hunkers. Her hair fell down around her shoulders in a loose tangle of knots, lending her a wild, possessed look. Most of the flesh of her skinny legs was exposed, because the black slip she wore – presumably one of Aunt Lyrica's – was bunched up at her thighs.

'Make you scream, make you cry, make you scream, make you cry…' she chanted, rocking back and forth on her heels and pulling at her hair. 'He won't let up until you die. Heart, eyes, soul, lies. He won't let up until you die.'

'What's wrong with her?' Calanthe said, touching my arm. 'What's she doing? Why's she saying those things?'

'How should I know?' I wasn't sure what chilled me more, the words she spoke or her behaviour. Also, I felt a spark of irritation that she should display such craziness in front of Calanthe. That she should embarrass me like this. I gripped the doorframe so hard that my fingertips hurt.

He won't let up until you die.

Who was she talking about?

My father?

A cockroach as large as the silver filigree pill box my mother kept in her handbag scurried across the back of my hand. I swallowed a scream, came over all lightheaded. Felt my knees buckle. Thought I might collapse against Calanthe.

'Who are you talking to, Aunt Jeanette?' Calanthe said, shattering the frenzied madness of the moment, but creating an equilibrium of nightmare-surreal which filled the house like fetid corpse breath.

The danger was as yet unseen, shouldn't even exist, but I could taste it. Breathe it. Calanthe had asked my mother a question that should never have been asked. Subsequently, my mother snapped out of her trance. She fell quiet and still, which was even scarier somehow. I could see the whites of her eyes in the gloom. Everything including time seemed to grind to a halt. Then the grating of metal against metal started up again. Soft and teasing behind me and Calanthe. I imagined the kiss of giant scissor blades skimming together, but didn't dare look to see if I was right. Didn't dare take my eyes off my mother. If I did, I thought I would fall into the insanity of some unseen hole within myself from which I could never crawl back out.

'He's here,' my mother said. 'Right behind you.'

Those words, so blunt, so matter-of-fact, stopped my heart. And the breath in my lungs was a painful load in my chest which I wanted to expel, but couldn't. I felt like I was free-falling from a great height, fear coursing through my veins. I'd never known such terror. Because even though my mother was behaving completely irrationally, in that moment I *knew* she was telling the truth. That someone was standing right behind us. Someone so heinous he would inspire nightmares in all parts of me, conscious and otherwise, forever.

Calanthe's hand found mine and together we turned our heads. Slowly, slowly. The silhouette of a man towered over us. So close I could feel his humid breath gushing down onto my face. Could smell whatever decay rotted his gums and festered inside his gastrointestinal tract. A distinctive farmyard reek of musky animal coat emanated from him too. So heady, I thought I might pass out. It was hard to make out any distinct features on the man's face. It was too dark. But his eyes were murky white orbs, and I saw what looked like the glint of metal as he closed his mouth, opened then closed, opened then closed.

My lungs let loose and I expelled every bit of air within them with a throat-scratching scream. The building shook its black coat and issued a whine in response, then light flooded the hallway, making the nightmarish figure disintegrate to nothing, and Aunt Lyrica barrelled out of her bedroom. 'What's going on?' she cried.

Neither Calanthe nor I could find the words to explain, but from her place in the shadows of the lounge, my mother said, 'Tom Dockin's here. He followed me.'

10

Catherine Hall

2019

I remember thinking Tom Dockin must be the name of my father. It seemed like a revelatory breakthrough, but one I wasn't happy to have discovered. Because if he was the ghoulishly large figure who'd stood behind me in the hallway stinking of bad breath and goat hair and who'd then vanished with the light, he truly must be a monster, just as Calanthe had said. But later during that night, back in 1997, when Aunt Lyrica had calmed my mother somewhat and got us girls back to bed, Calanthe told me the weird truth: that Tom Dockin was the bogeyman. Some Yorkshire legend with iron teeth.

Why iron? I'd asked.

Use your loaf, Calanthe said. Having metal teeth makes it easier to eat people.

That was the first time I'd ever heard of my mother's obsession with the bogeyman and it made me consider she might be bat shit crazy. After all, the bogeyman is someone who preys on children. A fabricated character from fables, put in place to discourage bad behaviour; a symbol of dire consequence.

But then, hadn't me and Calanthe seen him with our own eyes?

There was never part of me that doubted I had, yet Calanthe denied having seen anything. Trick of the light and Aunt Jeanette going looney tunes was all she'd insisted. She might have convinced me with her flippant dismissal of the bogeyman, if not for the stink he'd brought with him; because tricks of the light don't reek of hot animal pelt and rancid breath. I know what I saw. I know what I smelt.

Tom Dockin.

His name was a disturbing remembrance from the past. It sent shivers through me, churning my stomach and making me want to be sick. A great, solid, hulking shadow who must have lurked within the confines of my subconscious for years, manifesting in newer, scarier forms without me even knowing – till now. My mother's death and coming back to The Zoltan must have freed him from his captivity.

I considered that I should speak to Aunt Lyrica about it. Discover when and why my mother had become fixated with this metal-toothed folkloric fiend. But I couldn't think of a tactful way in which to do so. I had a suspicion Tom Dockin's hold ran deep and was rooted as far back as Eden House, the orphanage where Aunt Lyrica and my mother had grown up. The place she was so reluctant to talk about. Therefore, I couldn't see any suitable way in which to broach the subject.

It had just turned seven when I went to the kitchen. Aunt Lyrica was cooking sausages, bacon and black pudding, even though Dan from Room Two wasn't up yet. My stomach growled with hunger, but I felt too nauseous to eat. Didn't think I'd be able to keep anything down.

'Sleep okay?' Aunt Lyrica asked when she saw me. An uncharacteristic cloud of negative funk hung over her. A cobwebby tangle of sullenness.

'Yeah,' I said, seeing no point in troubling her further with my own bad thoughts. 'You?'

'Yeah.' I could tell she was lying too.

It was still dark outside, the sun yet to struggle over the

horizon where the sea meets the sky. When it did, I knew its light would banish the obscure memory of Tom Dockin from my immediate thoughts, albeit with wintry tones of wistfulness. By noon I'd be wondering: did he really visit?

It had been a long few days, emotionally exhausting. No wonder I was making shapes out of shadows and imagining sounds within the quietude of a large building occupied by myself, Aunt Lyrica, Kevin the dog and Dan the mysterious stranger who so enraptured me. Tom Dockin had appeared after Uncle Ged's funeral and again after my mother's. He was a figure of death. A symbol of forced change. He existed entirely in my head. That was all.

Wasn't it?

I took two jugs to the dining room, one half-filled with orange juice and the other half-filled with milk. As I set them down on the bureau next to boxes of cereal and a bowl of fresh fruit, I noticed Aunt Lyrica had changed the painting on the chimneybreast wall. I wasn't sure when she'd done it or why; it seemed like a quirky choice even by her standards. Far too random. Too odd. Hardly family friendly. It showed a dismembered hand cut from the arm above the wrist. Sympathetic brush strokes made the subject appear all too real, yet it was strangely feminine and graceful. The detached body part was poised as if animated, reaching out to the viewer, me, *Here, take my hand*. Where the arm should have been, swirls of cherry blossom bloomed. Pretty petals born of blood and tissue rose from the stump. The hand's nails were iridescent pink, like the inside of an oyster shell where parasites and foreign bodies get coated in nacre. A space for perfect pearls. The picture was a delicate, morbidly beautiful depiction of a gruesome subject: mutilation. Perhaps murder. Upon closer inspection I could see the tips of the nails were ragged, and black with collected dirt. A telling sign of struggle?

I couldn't imagine the chaos within Aunt Lyrica's headspace when she'd created it. Was she coming undone? Less emotionally stable than she'd have me believe?

As I studied more of the painting's lines and shading in careful detail, wanting to know what had happened to the amputee, an earwig crawled from beneath the canvas and trailed across the severed hand. An uninvited, repugnant guest, it belonged in the same soil which was beneath the hand's ragged nails.

Hurried footsteps in the hallway further startled me. I turned my head in time to see someone dart past the dining room. A blonde girl in Victoriana goth gear: flowing black velvet skirt and satin boned bodice with lace edging. She kept her head bowed, as if hoping to go unnoticed, unrecognised. But I knew that hair. Knew that dress sense.

Calanthe!

I was paralysed. Forgot how to breathe. A great tightness in my chest prevented me from calling out. But what would I have said, anyway?

The vampire in my room flinched, turned its head to the side. Eyes wide. Calanthe's back, it said. I think she's…

Dan appeared in the doorway. A vision of ordinariness in a grey knitted chunky jumper and blue jeans, no shoes, just white sports socks on his feet. Yet, there was something…

'Morning,' he said, smiling. 'Smells great down here.'

'Morning.' I smiled back, the reciprocal gesture too strained. I must have looked deranged; my thoughts whirring too much. Calanthe's back. Calanthe's back!

Dan seemed to notice. 'Is, um, everything okay?'

'Yeah…' I stumbled closer to the door, my heart soaring. With fear? Or hope? 'Did you see someone out there just now? A blonde girl.'

Dan glanced over his shoulders, checking the hallway

both ways, his expression one of clear bemusement. 'Nope, sorry. Didn't notice anyone.'

Had I been mistaken? Had I imagined Calanthe? Taken the image of her from archived memories and projected it onto the impossible, usually time-restrained screen space of now?

Or was I turning into my mother?

I squeezed my eyes shut and rubbed my temples, trying to massage away crazy thoughts. It didn't work. Calanthe was at The Zoltan. Right now. And I couldn't convince myself otherwise. The fleeting sight of her was burnt into my mind's eye.

That she'd looked as I remembered all those years ago at the time of her disappearance meant either her ghost had returned to The Zoltan in some state of purgatory or the building itself was showing stills from the summer of 2003, presenting snippets of her last days. Offering clues.

Clues?

What clues?

The vampire mewled like a kitten, a piteous sound that stabbed at my brain. Think, Catherine, think. The severed hand on the canvas behind me twitched, then tightened to a fist. My innards convulsed like I'd been gut-punched.

Oh Mother, why did you have to be crazy?

'Are you sure you're okay?' Dan said. He rubbed his chin. His hand was manly, fingernails tidy. No wedding band, but an indent where one had been.

'Yeah.' I struggled to find any more words than that with which to convince him. He was making me even more irritable. Perhaps because he didn't look right. When I'd seen him the day before I'd presumed he'd have hair beneath the woollen hat he'd worn. He didn't. His head was shaven close to his scalp. Not that it was any business of mine. What should it even matter?

Yet strangely, it did.

His eyes seemed friendly enough but impossible for me

to read with any amount of certainty, given that I was behaving madly and staring at him as I was. He skimmed past me and took a seat at the table nearest the window. As he did, I got a waft of his deodorant; masculine and clean.

'Looks like it's gonna be a total washout today.' Dan conveyed an air of casual confidence as he spoke. Seemed compelled to fill the awkward chasm I'd left gaping with my lack of social ease.

'Er, yeah.' I looked to the window, realised only now it was raining. Calanthe's here and she hated the rain. 'Can I get you any tea? Coffee?'

'Tea would be great, thanks.' Dan stretched to one side and eased his mobile phone from the pocket of his trousers. The Zoltan wasn't a terrible spot for signal, so if anyone was to call or send a message he'd probably receive it. He pressed the screen and tapped an app icon, then scrolled through what looked like a message thread which had the name Steve at the top.

I continued to stand by his table, all indecisive and curious. Afraid that if I didn't speak now, I never would. 'Did you, er, get any good pictures yesterday?'

Dan looked surprised that I should take an interest. That I should know. That I was still there.

'You talked to my aunt before you left,' I reminded him. 'You headed out with a camera.'

'Oh, yeah. I did. Went along to Sandsend.' He elaborated only that much. His eyes, slightly puffy from sleep or lack thereof, were suspicious. Again I sensed a connection of pasts entwined. There was something about him that pulled me in. Something more alluring than his voice. He was unpretentiously good-looking. Made me feel less than average and embarrassed about myself. Self-apologetic because I hadn't thought to put any lip gloss on or brush my hair before throwing it up in a messy bun. Someone like him would never look at someone like me,

I thought, not if I didn't make more of an effort.

'I'm Dan, by the way.' His expression conveyed subtle humour, and his smile seemed unforced. 'Dan Munro.'

Munro.

Good, I thought. He's a mountain, not a Hill. A Scottish mountain.

'I'm Cat,' I told him, not sure why. Was I deciding now of all times to recreate myself? Was I trying to sound more interesting? 'Cat Hall.'

'Sounds like a place I'd like to visit,' he said, causing a deep heat to rise to my cheeks. I felt the vampire stir. Inflate. Blood trickled through its thin, stringy veins.

'What do you mean?'

Dan picked up a sachet of sugar and fiddled with it. 'Cat Hall. It sounds like a place filled with big rooms and interesting heirlooms. A manor house belonging to some aristocratic widow who keeps cats for company. Two hundred at least. Sounds like somewhere I'd stay for a while.'

'Oh. I see.' I didn't at all, but my interest in him increased tenfold.

'Sorry.' Dan laughed. 'Sometimes I think aloud when really I shouldn't.'

'Don't worry, Cat Hall sounds great when you put it like that.' I laughed too. Relaxed a little. Felt some tension ease from my body. Was certain beyond any remaining sliver of doubt that I didn't know Dan Munro. At least, not from this lifetime. I imagined the hall from my dream but without my mother, Uncle Ged and Calanthe. Instead, Dan and I played tiddlywinks on the table and drank red stuff from pewter goblets.

'Right then, I'll get you a pot of tea,' I said, prompting myself to move away. To come undone from the mystifying draw of his eyes. To come unfastened from his attention, which I no longer wanted because I worried I might embarrass myself even more.

On the way to the kitchen Calanthe was nowhere to be seen. I checked on the stairs and in Aunt Lyrica's private lounge, but found nothing but the loud ticking of the wall clock above the fireplace. I remembered when Calanthe and I had stood in the lounge's doorway all those years ago, my mother hunkered on the floor and Tom Dockin standing behind us. Right there, on *that* patch of carpet. I was a grown woman now and logic told me the bogeyman couldn't possibly exist. And yet, and yet…

In the kitchen, Aunt Lyrica was loading bread into the toaster. She seemed to have perked up a little and was humming along to a power ballad on Smooth Radio. *Alone* by Heart. I decided not to mention Calanthe. Not yet. Not till I was certain she was here.

'Is he ready for breakfast?' Aunt Lyrica asked.

'Shit.' I palmed my forehead. 'Forgot to ask.'

'What're you like?' She shook her head in mild disparagement, but grinned. 'Still intrigued by him?'

'I told him my name is Cat,' I said, as though that was an acceptable answer.

Aunt Lyrica's grin widened. 'I'll take that as a yes then.'

'I don't know why I did it.' I turned my back to her and threw two tea bags into a stainless steel teapot, then filled it with boiling water from the kettle. Steam rose from the spout in confident, white swirls. This made me think about auras. Could Aunt Lyrica really see mine? Was it grey and shabby, as she'd said?

'I know why you did it,' Aunt Lyrica said. 'You're keen to explore a different aspect of yourself.'

'And what aspect would that be?'

'The one you're not familiar with.'

'Which is?'

'The great seductress.'

Ugh. I groaned. 'It's a little too early for that, isn't it?'

'Not when the feeling strikes.'

'Mustn't have struck very hard in that case.'

This time Aunt Lyrica groaned. 'Bloody hell, Cat, when was the last time you had a boyfriend? I mean, have you ever even had one?'

I shrugged. Didn't care to dwell on the answer to either of those questions. 'What's that got to do with me being Cat Hall instead of Catherine Hall?'

'Everything.' Aunt Lyrica crossed her arms over her chest, to make some pointed stand against me. Today she was wearing black skinny jeans and a red crushed velvet body. Every day a glamour day. 'No offence, but Catherine Hall's a bit of a wallflower.'

Wallflower?

Something like fear or quiet unease poked at my consciousness. Something I didn't want to explore. I exhaled loudly to express my disapproval. Wanted to ask how the hell she might presume to reach that conclusion. But I didn't, because of course she was right. I was a wallflower.

Wallflower.

There was that same dread, like the onset of fever. Creeping with hotness up my neck.

'Lighten up, for goodness' sake,' Aunt Lyrica said, laughing. 'I'm pulling your leg. You've been checking out the bloke in Room Two, so what? You're human. You need to remind yourself of that sometimes, love. Let yourself to have some fun, especially while you're still young.'

'Who says I don't have fun?'

Aunt Lyrica ignored the offer of confrontation. Decided not to shoot me down in flames. We both knew it was a weak challenge.

'Look, it's chucking it down outside,' she said, 'not exactly beach-friendly weather. Why don't you ask Dan what he's up to today? Or offer to go for a few drinks with him later.'

This time I laughed. 'You're getting entirely too carried

away. I don't like him. Not like that.'

'Fibber.'

'I don't. Besides, he might be married.'

'No ring.' Aunt Lyrica had noticed too.

'Doesn't mean he's not in a relationship.'

She raised her eyebrows. 'Only one way to find out.'

'Who's saying he'd want to do anything with me, anyway?'

'Ah, so you're scared of rejection?' She nodded, as if she'd understand! 'You put yourself down too much. I'll ask him for you, if you're too shy.'

'Oh, piss off.' I flashed her a quick two-fingered salute, picked up Dan's pot of tea and left the kitchen.

In the hallway I could still hear her laughing at my response. I looked to the stairs. Expected to see Calanthe standing halfway up, watching me through the wooden balustrade spindles, grinning. But she wasn't there.

No one was.

In the dining room, I put Dan's pot of tea on the table. He reached over to lift it and, as he did, a large centipede emerged from the dish of condiments at the centre of the table. It scurried across the white tablecloth like a defamation of Aunt Lyrica's cleanliness, then headed towards him. I watched it wide-eyed, not sure whether to swipe it away or try to gain Dan's attention so he might not see. But he didn't seem to notice, anyway. He poured tea into his cup while looking at the screen on his phone. The centipede's armoured body slipped past his left arm and disappeared behind his elbow. After adding milk to his cup, Dan stirred in sugar with a spoon, shifted in his seat, then leant back. He lifted his cup to his mouth and blew. Took a careful sip. The centipede was no longer on the table, I saw. Must have dropped to the floor.

'Are you, er, ready to order breakfast yet?' I said, my eyes still scanning the blankness of the tablecloth.

Dan looked up at me and winked. 'Aye, I'll have the full

works, please.'

The dismembered hand on the wall behind me beckoned, and the vampire shuddered on voluptuous red bedsheets in quiet ecstasy.

You'd look good on my walls.

I swear Dan's eyes were bluer than they'd been only moments before. Devilish almost. Maybe a trick of the increasing daylight. I sensed he was testing me somehow, revelling in my discomfort, my sheer awkwardness. I couldn't look away. Stood there gawping like an idiot. And only when the sound of something clattering in the kitchen coursed through the entire ground floor of The Zoltan was I able to break the spell.

'I'll be right back,' I said, darting away as nimbly as the centipede.

In the kitchen, while Aunt Lyrica plated up Dan's breakfast, I considered asking what she'd known about my mother during her final years. A subtle way perhaps of broaching the subject of Tom Dockin. I'd assumed my mother was happy, but now wasn't sure. Perhaps Patrick Hill hadn't cured her of Tom Dockin and the other demons that chased her (me included). After she and Patrick met, she'd transformed, both physically and mentally. Even if it was just an act, which I now suspected was the case. She'd smartened her appearance, taken pride in how she looked, and became outwardly normal. Definitely not the kind of woman anyone would suspect believed in the monsters and ghouls from kids' stories. But now I wasn't sure what her state of mind had been at any stage, nor whether the bogeyman had ever left her. Subsequently, I wondered if he'd ever leave me.

He won't let up until you die.

If Calanthe and I hadn't borne witness to my mother's breakdown on the night of Uncle Ged's funeral, would things be different now? It's impossible to know, but hard to discredit the idea. How much negative stuff, like traits and bad habits, rub off on us when we're young and impressionable? And how much of that shit sticks? In the end, I didn't broach any of these thoughts with Aunt Lyrica though. It still didn't feel like the right time.

I returned to the dining room with Dan's breakfast and almost dropped it on the floor when I saw the severed hand had gone from the chimneybreast wall. In its place was the canvas from the day before; the crimson rose and its shadow.

Where did it go? How can this be?

The hand's dirty fingernails scratched at my brain, its fingers probing, unravelling strands of my sanity like loose thread. Dan didn't seem to notice my upset, nor did he know that the amputated hand had never been on the wall. Had probably never existed. That there was something wrong with my mind. He was busy scrolling through his phone.

I set his breakfast before him, aware of the red rose and its dead-self leering at me. 'Are you, er, off out with your camera again today?' I said, as though everything was perfectly normal and the world hadn't started spinning the wrong way.

Dan looked up, as if surprised to see me there. But there was enough irritation in his eyes for me to know that he'd known I was there and hoped I'd leave him be. He shook his head. 'Not today.'

'Oh.' When he said nothing more, I moved off and pretended to tidy cereal boxes on the bureau, rejigging them then putting them back as they were. My head swam with disturbing images. Photographs of dismembered body parts. A mangled hand with cherry blossom flourishing at the wrist; tiny delicate flower heads sprouting from tiny severed arteries. A slender foot, bruised and ragged at the ankle where the flesh was torn. Individual fingers, bloody stumps. An amputated breast on a silver plate, rose-pink nipple intact. Erect.

Turning to Dan again, I had to know: 'Is photography a hobby of yours?'

He swallowed a mouthful of food, then said, 'Yeah, something like that.' He held his knife and fork upright on the table, and I had a fleeting image of his hands entwined with long blonde hair.

'Escapism?'

A light scratching came from the walls. Beneath the building's epidermis, I imagined beetle shells clicking together and the fingernails of severed fingers clawing against wooden joists. Dan didn't appear to hear it. He carried on eating. 'Suppose so.'

Scratch-scratch-scratch.

Too many nonsensical, macabre thoughts were threatening to send me over the edge of some inexcusable, ostentatious hysteria brought on by grief – because that's exactly what was causing these hallucinatory episodes, I decided. I had to ignore the delusions. Keep them in check. Keep busy. Not feed the madness. But still the scraping in the walls persisted. The red rose lingered in the background like a gunshot spatter of blood, looming in my peripheral vision like a suppressed memory. I imagined I could smell the pleasant sweat of Dan's body. In some other time…

The vampire moaned.

'Sorry,' I said, trying to ignore whatever beckoned behind the walls. 'I'm being a nuisance.'

'No, you're not.'

'Yes, I am. I should let you eat your breakfast in peace.'

Dan wafted a hand like he didn't care. And maybe he didn't. The mild annoyance had left his eyes. 'That's okay.'

I took his blasé pardon as an invitation to ask, 'What do you take pictures of?' Because it was something I felt I needed to know.

He puffed out his cheeks and loaded his fork. 'Anything

interesting, I suppose.'

'And what do you find interesting?'

He shrugged. 'Lots of things.'

He was hard to engage with, wasn't giving much away, but for reasons unclear I had to know. 'People?'

'Posed portraits, you mean?'

The floor buckled beneath me and the vampire sighed; I felt its weak breath breeze through my chest cavity like wind filtering into a forgotten crypt.

You'd look good on my walls.

But Dan was already shaking his head, shattering the concept of whatever it was I thought I'd almost discovered. 'I prefer landscapes and objects, if I'm honest. Interesting compositions.'

'Oh, okay.'

'I have done portraits,' he said, taking a drink of tea. 'But that was a long time ago.'

I turned to the canvas on the wall. The rose and its shadow had gone and the dismembered hand was poised, summoning me with a curled finger.

Come with me. I'll show you what it is you need to be shown.

11

Summer

2019

The train hurtled south, leaving Durham behind in a slurry of sleety wetness. Summer Hill could see the face of the woman opposite reflected in the window, superimposed on the changing grey, brown and dull green vista. She kept looking Summer up and down, didn't even try to conceal the fact. Summer didn't enjoy being ogled at the best of times, but today she felt paranoid that everyone knew just by looking at her that she'd run away. She clutched at the backpack in her lap, its contents heavy with physical and mental freight. Anxiety clawed at the underside of her skin, making her irritable and fidgety. She was convinced her dad would be at Whitby station, waiting. Hands balled into fists, resting on his hips, his dark eyes ablaze as he asked: And where the hell do you think you're going, young lady?

First thing that morning, he'd dropped her off at the bus station, telling her to go straight home after college. No playing silly buggers, he'd warned. You've got plenty of studying to be getting on with.

But Anna's mum is going to take us to the Metro Centre, Summer had said, the lie coming easily. She'd wanted to buy as much time as possible to make her getaway. It's late night opening and the Christmas decorations are up and there's a huge tree and some glittery reindeer suspended from the ceiling in one of the atriums.

But Patrick Hill was having none of it and, apparently, he thought building and developing friendships wasn't important for a sixteen-year-old. That stuff's frivolous, he'd said. Friends come and go, as do silly decorations. You need to concentrate on your grades. Studying is more important, and Christmas is certainly no excuse. Be home on time.

God forbid she was to have a boyfriend.

Summer had got on a different bus to the one that would have taken her to college. She'd gone to Catherine's house instead, arriving unannounced with the backpack she'd packed full of her stuff and the flimsy foundation of a plan she'd concocted in her head. Nothing solid. But her sister hadn't been home. All the blinds were pulled shut in her two-bedroom terraced house and the drive empty. Catherine might have popped out to the shops or to an appointment, but the house looked too shut-up for that. Too deserted. Even the gate to the back garden had been padlocked.

Catherine had gone away.

Summer could have called to find out where, but she found phone calls awkward and too anxiety-inducing. She didn't want to risk Catherine dobbing her in either. Besides, she'd turned her phone off. Didn't want her dad calling. Also, she wasn't wholly certain he didn't track her whereabouts with it. She needed to be careful. Play it safe. He'd be furious when he discovered that not only had she skipped college and run away, but she'd stolen from his wallet too.

Since her mum's death, Summer found her dad even more overbearing than usual. She was the sole focus of his domineering personality. The only one he could control. Zara, his other daughter from his previous marriage – fully grown and self-sufficient – only ever saw him twice a year, if that. Summer realised, therefore, that she would endure Patrick Hill's egotism alone. Already she couldn't stand it.

She'd hoped to shack up at Catherine's for a few nights, to get her head in order and decide what she wanted to do with her life. At present she was studying for A-levels at college in subjects she wasn't passionate about. Her dad was pushing her to go to law school, whereas what she really wanted was to be a hairdresser or beautician. She wanted to run her own business one day. A trendy salon. Boutique vibes. Ultra chic. But apparently that wasn't good enough for any daughter of Patrick Hill's. He'd made it clear he wasn't prepared to support her in the life she wanted. Wouldn't listen to her hopes and dreams. Deemed them 'fluffy-headed'. You'll thank me later for setting you on the right track, he'd said, and giving you the encouragement to pursue a decent profession.

As much as he said he wanted her to be an independent, high-flying career woman, he treated her like a child. Stifled her. Made out she was as fragile as a fine china bird that might break if not nestled in his hands. Summer often wondered if that's how everyone saw her, even Catherine. A precious, pretty thing that needed protecting and sheltering at all times.

Well, she'd prove them all wrong.

Sixteen years separated Summer and Catherine, which was a hell of a lot of time in terms of sibling kinship. Even though she'd grown up with Catherine loosely in her life, there was no special bond between them. Which is why, she thought, she wouldn't feel too guilty for doing what she had in mind…

'Tickets, please.' A guard about the same age as her dad was standing in the aisle, hands on hips. His watery, bloodhound eyes lingered on Summer for longer than she was comfortable with, assessing the backpack in her grip as if he knew what it contained.

The woman opposite, already poised, ready for

inspection, handed her ticket over. Summer rummaged in her coat, mildly panicked because she couldn't remember where she'd put hers. It was in a zipped inner pocket, folded in half. She passed it to the guard, her hands clammy, then watched as he checked its validity. All the while her heart thumped in case he told her that actually she'd need to go with him because her dad had reported her missing and he was waiting along with some police officers at the next station to take her home. But he didn't. He said, 'Ta, love,' then gave the ticket back and moved off.

Summer relaxed back into her seat and resumed looking out the window. The sprawling landscape beyond was like an illusion. How far from home would her tether reach? This was the furthest she'd been unaccompanied. Her legs ached beneath the weight of the backpack. She shuffled her feet, tried to rearrange its bulk, but it did no good. Still it bore down on her. Its contents and what she meant to do horrified her, because…

The woman opposite was staring again, eyes narrowed. I know what you have in that bag, Summer imagined her saying, and what you plan to do with it, you horrible little shit.

Summer scowled at her own reflection. Pretended to watch the brooding clouds which hung over them no matter how fast the train went. Inside the unassuming nylon shell of the backpack was information Summer knew Catherine would want. And Summer was willing to hand it over, but only in exchange for a decent price.

So there, she thought. You ARE a horrible little shit.

For as long as Summer remembered, there had been tension between Catherine and their mother. But whenever Summer tried to broach the subject, her mum had fallen quiet. Refused to talk. Become withdrawn. Moody, even. Summer had dared to ask once or twice who Catherine's dad was, because in in her mind she couldn't understand why she had one but Catherine didn't. But her mum had never given an answer. Not even a hint.

But now Summer knew. She had revelatory information. Straight from the horse's mouth too.

Just days after her mum had died, when her dad was distracted by funeral plans, Summer had nosed through some of her mum's stuff in the attic. Amongst bundles of ancient magazines and clothes and boxes of photographs (circa the Patrick Hill years, nothing before), she'd found some diaries. Most were the boring ramblings of a housewife, or at least a pretence at being just that. But the earlier ones when her mum was much younger; some entries in those were much more… bizarre. Downright disturbing, in fact. Summer wasn't sure what to think about all that had been documented in spidery black ink. Nor what her mum's mental state had been when she'd written them. Whatever the case, one diary addressed the mystery of Catherine's paternal bloodline. Summer knew the name of her sister's biological father. She wasn't sure if it was the ethical thing to do to bring the journal to Catherine's attention, because ignorance was surely bliss. No good would ever come from knowing this truth.

But then, didn't Catherine have a right to the truth? Or at least to decide what to do with the information their mother had written all those years ago.

If the diary should belong to anyone now, it was Catherine. And Summer needed money. So, even though it was a little unfair and morally questionable, it was a win-win situation. Hell, who was she kidding? What she proposed to do was grossly unfair and morally atrocious. But still they'd both get what they wanted.

As soon as Summer had seen that Catherine's house was locked up and vacant, she'd suspected her sister had gone to Whitby. Catherine didn't have many friends, certainly none that she'd stay with. She was a creature of habit, liked her own surroundings, the familiarity of her own walls and furniture. So the only logical explanation was that she'd gone to stay with Aunt Lyrica.

Aunt Lyrica's B&B was on Whitby's West Cliff. Summer couldn't remember exactly where. She'd visited The Zoltan only a handful of times, last summer being the last. Her mum had pleaded with her dad to take them all out for the day, and that's where they'd gone. It was a forbidding red-brick Victorian building, that was all Summer could recall. Perhaps that and the fact the hallway felt like a rabbit's warren; dark and dingy, leading to too many unseen rooms that might as well be underground. The smell of too many people was ingrained in all surfaces. They hadn't stayed long. A quick, awkward cuppa in the kitchen, because her dad had never made a secret about disliking Aunt Lyrica. Brings out the worst in you, Jeanette, he'd once said. The less you see of her, the better.

Afterwards, Summer had walked along the promenade with her mum and dad. A blustery but warm day. Lots of people and dogs. She remembered her dad buying a red sugar dummy from one of the confectionery booths along the seafront and giving it to her as though she was six. She hadn't complained though. She'd wanted that sugar dummy as much as any six-year-old. Now, Summer couldn't imagine him buying anything for her ever again. He'd be apoplectic. Especially when he discovered she'd run off to Aunt Lyrica's. Summer wasn't sure what her dad founded his dislike for her mother's sister upon, but there were so many things he disliked it would be pointless trying to guess.

She couldn't hope to share anywhere near the level of closeness Catherine did with their aunt, for which she was jealous. She felt like she'd missed out on a lot. Just as her mother and Aunt Lyrica were close in age, so too were Catherine and Aunt Lyrica's daughter, Calanthe

Black – the supposed wild child who'd run away in the nineties, on the very day Summer was born. Apart from speculative details that felt too much like legends from a well-thumbed library book, Summer didn't know much else about her cousin; only that she'd, apparently, looked a lot like Summer herself.

Whatever the real story of Calanthe Black, Summer thought she'd had the right idea: run away and don't look back.

12

Catherine Hall

2019

There was a break in the rain mid-morning, so I took Kevin for a walk down to the harbour area. Aunt Lyrica asked if I wanted company, but I declined her offer. Needed time alone to think. To contemplate all that had happened since I arrived at The Zoltan. I couldn't ignore the fact I was seeing things: Calanthe, Tom Dockin and changing wall art.

Were the hallucinations a result of grief or something much worse?

Inherited madness.

That's what I needed to reflect upon.

With all my heart and soul, I wanted to believe stress brought on by my mother's death had induced each delusion, but deep down I didn't think this could be the case because in truth I hadn't suffered. Perhaps implicitly, but not for the reason people might expect. Since my mother's death, I hadn't cried. Not once. I wasn't drowning in sorrow. Wasn't driving myself crazy with *what ifs* and regret, wishing I'd done things differently. Because I didn't.

During her final days I'd visited a few times, enduring the pained silences and awkward glances, imagining she looked even more pained because I was there. I hadn't gone to show face and offer empty words of comfort, owed to some meaningless obligation society expected of me because I was her daughter, but because I held on to some hope that she might divulge the information I'd waited my whole life to hear: my father's name. But she held firmly to that secret and now she was dead. I grieved only that lost information. Maybe this sounds harsh, unfeeling perhaps, but my mother and I had never been close. Therefore I didn't believe I was in mourning for her at all, so reasoned bereavement couldn't be the reason for the alarming hallucinations my subconscious now indulged. I'd handled none of the funeral arrangements and had no cause to concern myself over possessions or inheritances, because nothing was coming my way. Also, my day-to-day life hadn't altered at all. I didn't have to live in the house where her absence was now a void. I'd moved out of the Hill household as soon as I was eighteen, so my own home life was just as quiet and regular as it had been for the past fourteen years. There was no change to my daily routine. So how could the death of someone I was obliged to love mean much at all?

Don't get me wrong, I could have loved my mother properly if she'd given me the chance. But she hadn't nurtured the biological bond between us. Had probably killed it outright when I was born. Most likely way before that time even. When she first discovered I was a real... thing.

My mother's madness, now that's a different beast altogether. Inherited traits don't need any kind of emotional involvement from either party. We had a chromosomal bond, and that was all that was required. Perhaps a bit of suggestion too. Goodness knows she projected her craziness onto me enough when I was a kid. Especially the night she introduced me to the bogeyman.

I'm surprised my mother didn't spout Tom Dockin gabble on her deathbed. Mind you, maybe she did. I wasn't there. I couldn't know what final words she spoke.

If she imparted any confessions or slipped away peacefully, only Patrick Hill will know. He hasn't spoken to me of anything I might want to hear. About anything at all, in fact.

Does it sound as though I hated my mother?

I didn't. I was simply indifferent to her. Had learned to stop vying for her attention and craving approval at an early age. I knew she must have her reasons for being distant. Resentment, at a guess. Because my father, whoever he was, must have done something unforgivable. It must have been something terrible for that hurt to have extended to me. But what did that make me?

An accidental monster?

A parasite?

The seafront was bitterly cold; the wind swiping inland with wintry blasts. Kevin and I dawdled then hurried in intermittent bursts, as though we kept forgetting we were meant to be somewhere then suddenly remembering.

Kevin stopped to sniff at railings, lampposts and other stationary fixtures which other dogs had urinated on, sometimes leaving his own mark in response. The canine equivalent of social media. The streets were fairly inactive. The bandstand was a deserted black skeleton, ruminating memories of the hundreds of visitors who'd fleshed it out all summer. The arcades were redundant and eerily quiet in the wake of those same high-season thrill seekers. There were people milling about, of course. Tourism never really dies in a place where Dracula once landed within the pages of a book. But it had eased up considerably.

Everything was the same, but different. Same colours, different mood. Or was it same mood, different colours? I couldn't put my finger on it. It seemed like a whole lifetime ago when I used to follow Calanthe like a shadow through the same cobbled streets. At every shop and café window I expected to see her reflection staring back, her ghost having followed me this time. She was too showy in life to lie low for so long, therefore Aunt Lyrica's assertion seemed somehow right: Calanthe was dead. Suspended in time at the age of sixteen. Unable to move on because…

My dearest Wilhelmina, that thing you did… well, it was the most impressive thing you ever did.

There was a loud blast of a horn right behind me. I spun round and saw a bin lorry bearing down on me, its ruddy-faced driver glaring through the windshield. He gestured me out of the way with impatient hands, shaking his head. I was standing in the middle of the road. Hadn't heard the rumble of the lorry's engine. Kevin was looking up at me as if to say: Are you trying to get us killed? I held my hand up to the lorry driver in apology and scampered to the pavement. I imagined Calanthe laughing at me.

Touché.

By the time Kevin and I got back to The Zoltan, I'd done plenty of thinking and had mostly convinced myself I was well on the way to madness. On board the Jeanette Hill Crazy Express. My ticket had been punched, my seatbelt buckled, next stop: Out of Your Fucking Mind. I hung my coat on a peg in the back porch and saw an unfamiliar coat hanging amongst the others there. I hadn't noticed it earlier. A bright red padded parka with a luxuriously furred hood, like the fur of a timber wolf. Not the kind of coat you'd miss. It was at that point I noticed voices coming from the kitchen.

We had a visitor.

Kevin ran ahead of me and pawed the kitchen door open, his tail already wagging. I saw Aunt Lyrica at the sink with the kettle in her hand.

'Oh Cat,' she said, turning and smiling. 'You're just in time for a cuppa. Someone's come to see us.'

I stepped into the kitchen. My heart lurched. Summer, my kid sister, was sitting at the dining table. She looked up from petting Kevin who was fussing around her legs. 'Hi.'

'Hi.' I pulled out the chair farthest from her and plonked down.

Today, Summer looked astoundingly like Calanthe. So much so, I wondered if The Zoltan's lighting added to the effect or if Calanthe's ghost had wrapped itself around her in approval.

Aunt Lyrica grabbed a third mug from the cupboard and set about making tea. 'Isn't it a nice surprise?'

Certainly a surprise.

The vampire's chest rattled with newborn infection.

'How did you get here?' I asked Summer, my eyes widening in feigned interest. God, she was so beautiful. So much like the past. My fingers and hands began to burn and itch in the kitchen's warmth. I scratched at them, making red lines in the mottled skin.

'On the train.' There was something sheepish about her; a reluctance to meet my gaze.

'Was the journey okay?'

'Yeah. Fine.' She shrugged and fiddled with the fur behind Kevin's ears, eyes downcast.

'Are you planning on staying long?'

'At least a couple of nights, I should hope,' Aunt Lyrica said, hammering home the fact that this crucial detail hadn't yet been decided. 'She can have Calanthe's room.'

Calanthe's room!

My heart heaved again, and I felt sick with something. Jealousy? Dread?

Why did you come here? I wanted to ask. You had Mother, wasn't that enough that you now have to have Aunt Lyrica?

'Isn't it lovely that you're both here at the same time?' Aunt Lyrica said, chinking the three mugs with a teaspoon as she stirred milk into tea.

No. Absolutely not.

I closed my eyes, trying to ignore the pulsing headache that was mounting at my temples. Beetle legs ticked somewhere close by. Inside my head? I squeezed the bridge of my nose. This wasn't how I'd envisaged things.

Summer glanced up and smiled, as though she could hear my thoughts. She looked pleased with herself. Her flawless face like a peachy rose.

Why was she here?

Dan. Something about Dan and his camera sprung to mind. Photos of dismembered appendages and limbs, flashing white lights.

What did any of it mean?

Snip snip. Snip snip. The sound of metal slicing against metal grated inside my head like a guillotine. Iron teeth riveted to bleeding, black gums. The smell of horsehair.

You might not see him, but he's definitely here, my mother had said in the great hall of my dream.

I'm Mina Murray, I thought. My future husband is away on business. Transylvania.

Didn't know you had it in you, Calanthe said, blood on her top lip.

Me neither.

Perhaps at the end the little things may teach us most.

All those details. Yes. The small things we overlook.

But what about the big things we hide?

My lungs needed air but I no longer had the function to inhale. Couldn't breathe.

Hhh.

Hhh.

Hhh.

Aunt Lyrica turned to me, her brow crumpling. 'Is everything okay, love?'

Summer eyed me as though I was a mental patient.

In. Out. In. Out.

Breeeathe.

'Yeah.' I said, my voice a thin wheeze. 'I'll be fine.'

The vampire wheezed louder. 'Think I might be coming down with something. Came over a bit funny, that's all.'

Aunt Lyrica put a cup of tea before me, her face showing mild concern. 'You should take it easy for the rest of the day.'

'Maybe.'

Her mouth scrunched to one side, and she patted me on the shoulder. Good girl. Then she turned to Summer and said, 'I'm popping to the supermarket this afternoon, love, would you like to come? We can get some fresh air and do some catching up.'

The words twisted in my heart like a knife.

'Sounds good, yeah.' Summer's voice was all black cherry perfect, just like Calanthe's had been.

My fingernails bit into my palms.

That thing you did. That thing you did.

It was the most impressive thing.

Calanthe's laughter shook free from the walls. No one else heard, except maybe Kevin.

Later, when Aunt Lyrica and Summer left The Zoltan, I watched from the dining-room window as they walked down Crescent Avenue together, Summer's red coat draining the colour from everything else. After they'd passed out of sight, I waited till the dull colours returned to brickwork, pavement, parked cars and sky. Then I raced to Calanthe's room. I didn't know what I expected to find, but had a compulsion to see what my little sister had brought with her.

A large hiking backpack had been dumped on the double bed, its main compartment open and clothes spilling out on the floral bedspread. I eyed it for a few seconds, as though it might be a sleeping dog that might bite if disturbed. When it didn't move, I prodded it with probing fingers and unzipped the large pocket on the front. Inside was a toiletry bag containing a tin of deodorant, a pink toothbrush, a full tube of toothpaste, a blue comb and a black elastic hair bobble. Nothing in the least bit interesting.

Next I rummaged through the clothes already on the bed: t-shirts, jumpers and leggings. All standard stuff. Smaller than anything I'd ever hope to get into. Then I tipped the backpack upside down, emptying the rest of its contents. Three more tops fell out, followed by five pairs of plain cotton knickers and four rolled up pairs of brightly coloured socks. One of the sock parcels bounced to the floor. I stopped it from rolling under the bed with my foot, then stooped to pick it up. I felt something crinkle inside as I did, so I pulled the socks apart and discovered a roll of twenty-pound notes huddled amongst embroidered dancing unicorns. Ten in total. Notes, not unicorns. I wondered if the money was stolen or taken from personal savings. Might even be pocket money, because who knew what funds Patrick Hill gave his daughter.

Intrigued by the discovery, I opened another sock parcel; this one lemon, with lilac fairy cakes. Inside I found nothing. But in the third ball of socks – pastel blue, with cartoon pugs – I found a credit card with the name MR PATRICK HILL on the front. It was at this point I suspected Summer had run away from home. Had probably stolen the cash from Patrick too. I eyed the final pair of rolled up socks; pink, with llamas.

Would I find anything else?

I pulled them apart hoping I would, and felt a deviant thrill when a small pouch fell onto the bed. Inside the clear plastic was a strip of small, white paper squares, each with a red love heart print.

Stolen money *and* drugs?

A flutter of laughter rose from my stomach. It didn't reach my mouth, my tongue suppressing it at the back of my throat.

How very much like Calanthe you are, little sis.

The fact the backpack had been opened but not properly unpacked made me wonder if Summer had taken something from it already. Something that might have been more obvious to find than the treasures in her socks.

But what?

I dropped to my knees and checked under the bed. Found nothing but boxes filled with Calanthe's stuff: sketch books, shoes and accessories. Loads of junk that should have been binned a long time ago. Next I had a quick rummage in the wardrobe. Everything I sifted through there was Calanthe's too. An entire rail of her clothing that Aunt Lyrica refused to get rid of because *she might come back*.

I wondered if I should call Patrick, to let him know Summer was here and that she'd stolen his credit card. He'd probably come and pick her up. Take her away.

'But why would you do that?' Calanthe's voice startled me.

I whirled round and found her lying on the bed on her side. Her curved body a sublime S. She was a real flesh and blood vision of the way she'd been all those years ago, nothing ghostly about her at all. She was wearing a black spandex mini dress and fishnet tights. Her blonde hair a wild mane, always her crowning glory.

'Aren't you intrigued about why she came?' she said when I didn't reply.

I still couldn't speak. Felt the impossible push and pull of air, as though the room might inhale me.

'Of course you are.' She held a hand to her black-lipped mouth to cover a smirk. It was then I noticed her fingers and thumb were missing. Taken from just below the knuckle, each was little more than a gory stump. The rest of her hand was slick with old, tarry blood. Blood which had transferred to the floral bedspread. And Summer's clothes.

Oh God.

'What happened to your fingers?' I said, my voice a horrified whine. I stumbled backwards, but the room continued to swell and deflate, keeping me upright. The light from the window no longer seemed real. And maybe it wasn't. It was too yellow for sunlight. Too warm for winter.

'Never mind that.' Calanthe sat up, still bearing that grin. A stringy black insect emerged from the neckline of her dress and ran up her throat, along her jawline and disappeared behind her ear, into her hair. She didn't seem to notice. She swiped at Summer's belongings with her left hand, which was still intact, and said, 'Aren't you going to put everything back the way you found it, before my mum and Summer come back?'

I looked at the ransacked backpack. Felt sick with the thought of stepping closer to the bed. Of getting Calanthe's blood on my skin – or rather, not being able to get it off again. But I had no choice. Calanthe was right. I had to tidy up.

I folded and repacked Summer's clothes, somehow remembering how to breathe while pretending not to notice the dark whorls of blood on my fingers. Calanthe watched me. Made no attempt to help. She cradled her chin in the palm of her mutilated hand, her big blue eyes alight with some unshared dark humour.

When I was done, she gestured to the wardrobe and said, 'Why don't you take my cloak?'

The words made little sense. They poured from her mouth like a language that relied on too many consonants. Her voice was too clicky, not mulling vowels over enough.

'The velvet cloak,' she urged. 'The one you always wanted for yourself. You loved it, didn't you? It's as heavy as a moonless night and just as black. Can you remember how you used to ask if you could wear it all the time?'

'You always said no.'

Calanthe laughed. 'It's no use to me now though, is it? Why don't you take it? Go to the clifftops and watch for the *Demeter* sailing in from the sky.'

'No thanks.'

'Suit yourself.' Calanthe rolled onto her back and looked up at the ceiling. Squinted at whatever she could see there. 'Summer can have it instead.'

My fingers flexed and I stormed to the wardrobe, yanking open the doors. There at the end of the rail was the hooded cloak. I fingered its velvety black folds, then slipped it from its hanger. Held it to my face and sniffed. It didn't smell of anything. Perhaps The Zoltan was already so ingrained with Calanthe's scent I was too used to it to notice anymore.

'All right,' I said, draping the heavy material over my arm. 'I'll take it.'

Calanthe sat upright, dangling her legs over the edge of the bed, and laughed. 'Poor Wilhelmina, you never belonged, did you?'

No. No, I didn't.

I left the room, closing the door behind me, strangely accepting of the fact I'd seen my dead cousin. Even more accepting of her gift to me. In Room One, I whipped the white waffle dressing gown from the bed, casting it to the floor like an offensive rag, then lay Calanthe's cloak in its place.

There. The vampire felt much healthier already.

13

Lyrica Black

2019

As Lyrica and Summer walked along Skinner Street towards Flowergate, the cutting wind spat spots of rain in their faces. A prelude of what was to come? The sky was an expanse of steely grey turbulence above them, stretching right out to the North Sea, accumulating more rain (or snow) after the downpour earlier that day. It looked swollen and bruised, almost ready to burst.

With each step and the subsequent rub of her jeans, Lyrica was mindful of the welt on the back of her legs from the night before. Was still trying to fit some logical explanation to the incident as she remembered it, but wasn't able to. A vivid nightmare couldn't wield physical afflictions. Nothing so distinct as the thin, painful line of Mr Birchwood, in any case. She could only presume the spirit of Sister Gregory had gained strength in the shadows.

But what was the significance?

Why now?

'You must miss her a lot,' she said, linking her arm through Summer's. Needing the contact. The closeness. A part of Jeanette to cling to.

'Yeah. It's strange.' The fur trim on Summer's hood concealed her face. She kept looking straight ahead. 'With Mum not being there, the house is so weird.'

'Quiet, you mean?'

'Not really. Just… empty of her. And Dad's in my face all the time.'

'I'm sure he doesn't mean to be.' Though Lyrica meant no such thing. Could imagine Patrick Hill was always keen to get in people's faces. A time like now wasn't appropriate for anything less than civility though, sniping and back-biting would help no one. 'He'll be hurting too. All you can do is to be there for each other.'

'Hmmm.'

Lyrica stiffened, sensing a rift she hadn't picked up on before. 'He knows you're here, doesn't he?'

Summer turned her head and smiled. 'Yeah, of course.'

She bore such a striking resemblance to Calanthe – same hair, eyes and build, albeit slightly different nose structure and mouth – the likeness made Lyrica almost too afraid to look for very long. Because what if the slight differences became less different, like when you think about a word too much and it becomes a strange thing that doesn't sound right or make much sense, they ended up becoming the same, and Summer was suddenly Calanthe, only not?

Personality wise, Summer displayed more of Jeanette's reserved nature, wasn't as self-assured as Calanthe, so Lyrica reckoned she'd be able to tell the difference if the subtle differences in Summer's face became the same. Few people possessed Calanthe's level of confidence. She'd been a drama queen through and through; the world her film set and everyone else an extra alongside her starring role. Perhaps it had been Lyrica's mistake to instil too much independence in the girl, trying to compensate for her own crappy childhood. All she'd wanted was for Calanthe to have a wonderful life. For her to be untouchable.

But where was she now?

Lyrica shuddered against Summer, mother's instinct

reaffirming the ephemeral but persistently recurring perception that her daughter was dead. A spidery inkling which lurked in every deserted street, empty room and unvoiced reply. Subtle, but as strong as any physical ache.

A shush-shushing sound behind, like heavy material billowing, made Lyrica's limbs stiffen. Could be a flag blowing in the wind, she supposed. Or a shop's fabric canopy trying to break loose from its metal bonds.

Whatever it was, in her head it was black.

She glanced over her shoulder. Saw nothing obvious, but a feeling of dread crept over her, cold and fierce like spectral hands grasping and clawing at her skin, and the memory of Sister Gregory's voice taunted her: Tom Dockin ate your eyes years ago. You've been blind to everything ever since.

What am I not seeing?

'How long is Catherine staying with you?' Summer asked.

'I'm not sure, love.' Lyrica noticed a flicker of something in her niece's eyes. Couldn't quite determine what it was. 'For as long as she needs to, I suppose. I don't think she knows herself.'

'I wish I could stay longer.' Summer came to a stop outside a second-hand jewellery store, its window display filled with old, quirky necklaces, bracelets and rings. Dying fairy lights trimmed each velveteen tray of jewellery. Strips of cotton wool edged the inside window sill, pretending to be snow. And a Santa Claus figurine beamed from a plastic face that was probably moulded in the eighties.

'There'll be plenty of opportunity for you to come and visit again next year,' Lyrica said, squeezing her niece's arm. 'Whitby's lovely in the summer. You can come and stay with me during the holidays if you like.'

The harsh sound of material folds slapping together returned, making Lyrica startle. She peeked over her shoulder. Glimpsed a tall black figure zip out of view into the recessed entrance of the shop next door.

A shopper, that's all.

'Look at that.' Summer, oblivious to Lyrica's torment, pressed her finger against the window, pointing to a fine chain necklace with a sterling silver rose pendant attached to it. Pieces of Whitby jet inlaid the rose's petals. 'Isn't it lovely?'

'Looks like something Calanthe would have worn,' Lyrica said, distractedly. During the past week, a prickly notion that something bad would happen had wrapped around her bones like tendrils of weeds. And in grief's mulchy shade, those weeds were growing with fastidious speed, tightening and pinching. Almost up to her throat. She thought she might choke on them soon.

'It's only a tenner,' Summer said.

Lyrica forced a smile. She wasn't fond of second-hand jewellery, was superstitious enough to think when you bought someone else's precious stones and metals you took on whatever problems they'd had. But it didn't seem right to pass this personal unease on to her niece. 'Why don't you get it?'

'Nah.' Summer frowned and started to move away. 'I don't have enough money with me.'

'Then I'll get it for you.' Lyrica reached into her handbag and pulled out a ten-pound note. 'My treat.'

Summer grinned, the gap between her top front teeth wider than Calanthe's had been. She accepted the money, seeming somehow suddenly childlike. Lyrica's heart ached. The bell above the door chimed like Christmases past, even the bad ones, especially the bad ones, as Summer bundled inside the shop. Lyrica stayed where she was at the window, stamping her booted feet and huddling her arms across her chest to keep warm. She checked over her shoulder and watched an elderly couple walk past on the other side of the road. A blessed scene of beige and other neutral-toned normality. No black figures creeping.

When she turned to face the window again, Lyrica saw the shop assistant taking the rose pendant from the window. The woman was youngish with short black hair and gaunt features. She said something then laughed. Summer laughed too. Lyrica caught sight of her own reflection. She looked wired and fraught. Needed to relax.

You should probably pray that he doesn't come for her. The unexpected voice of Sister Gregory was so abrupt in her head, Lyrica grasped the window ledge to stay upright. It wasn't a resurfacing memory of something the nun had once said. This was different. It was as though Sister Gregory had invaded her mind-space, projecting thoughts into her own.

Lyrica felt watched. She whirled round.

A silver car drove past, its tires shushing on the wet road. Its driver, a middle-aged man, gave her a passing glance. There was a family of four walking towards her from the corner of Skinner Street, and in the opposite direction the elderly couple were almost at the bottom of the bank. There was no one else about. Not that she could see.

Sister Gregory laughed and said, because you're blind to everything.

Where then? Lyrica clamped her jaw, afraid she might cry out in terrified frustration. Where are you?

Then she saw. Behind Summer in the dusty shadows of the second-hand shop stood a familiar figure swathed in black. A predator weighing up its prey. The old nun, slowly, teasingly, turned her corpse-grey face and grinned, all the blackness of mashed beetles forming that wicked smile.

You aren't real, Lyrica insisted, imagining her bones were calcifying because her arms and legs were too rigid. You're nothing but a consequence of my anxiety. Mine. You belong to me.

Are you sure about that, mother pig? The old nun's lips didn't move, but Lyrica could hear the gravelled mocking all too clearly as if she was standing right next to her. Every click of her rotten palate and the wetness of her black tongue forming those words.

And Tom Dockin won't let up, not until you die, Sister Gregory said. You of all people should know that already. And now this little piggy just came to market. Her arm extended like a spiky shadow in the gloom, her fingers seeking to snatch Summer.

He'll eat her fingers and toes one by one. Sister Gregory cackled. Oink, oink.

Lyrica barrelled into the shop. Watched as the area behind Summer dissolved into a straightforward grey gloom. Nothing more, nothing less. She exhaled with relief, but the panic within her wasn't quelled. Because this wasn't over.

'Is everything okay?' Summer said, turning to leave, a gift bag in her hand and look of alarm on her face.

'Yeah.' Lyrica scanned the shop again, ignoring the disdainful looks the shop assistant gave her. Sister Gregory was nowhere. 'It's spitting on to rain, that's all,' she said. 'We'd better hurry.'

'Oh wait,' Summer said, reaching out and brushing Lyrica's shoulder. 'There's something on your coat.'

'What?'

'I dunno. Some sort of bug.' Summer pointed to the floor. A cockroach scuttled past Lyrica's feet to the pavement outside.

Click-click-click.

Lyrica imagined the snakes in the walls of The Zoltan stirring.

14

Catherine Hall

2019

Downstairs, the phone rang and rang. A persistent clangour that hurt my head. Each shrieking peal raked up the walls and through the floorboards with a rhythmic doggedness, then drilled through my skull. It wouldn't stop. I dragged myself off the bed and lumbered down to the hallway, expecting to find Calanthe waiting there, her gored hand bleeding on the floor, her other pointing to the phone: Aren't you gonna answer it, Wilhelmina?

But she wasn't there.

No one was. Just the black corded telephone sitting on the sideboard, its shrillness more aggressive at such close range. I watched it for a while. Suspicious of whoever was on the other end. When it continued to ring, the person refusing to be ignored, I picked up the receiver. 'Hello?'

There was a brief silence, then a man's voice said, 'Lyrica?'

'No.'

'Oh. It is The Zoltan though?'

'Yes.' I closed my eyes, rubbed my lids and sighed. I recognised that pompous voice. 'Patrick.'

'Yes, um, how did you…?' For the briefest of moments, he sounded confused. Then enlightened. 'Ah, Catherine.'

'Yes.'

'Right, well listen, Catherine…'

Here we go. You listen to me, blah blah blah. His voice was a rolling car, no handbrake, the words too forced with his usual brashness for me to want to take any notice. Not till he said, 'So is she there? Is Summer at The Zoltan?' His thinly veiled panic confirmed my theory. Summer had run away from home. He didn't know where she was!

In the subsequent silence, as he waited for my response, I heard the *snip snip snip* of Tom Dockin's teeth grating together.

You might not see him, but he's here.

'Well?' Patrick urged.

'No,' I said. Which wasn't an outright lie. Summer was still out with Aunt Lyrica.

The vampire chuckled, and I surreptitiously roared with laughter inside myself. Now you listen to me, Patrick. 'Is that all?'

'Well, if you see her or hear from her…' he said.

'Yeah, I'll let you know.' I hung up. Stared at the phone for a while longer. Wondered if I really was coming down with something. Flashes of cold raced around my body in relays of hypothermic chills, but I also felt hot to the point of feverish, and a crow's talon of pain dug into my cerebral cortex with a blackness that threatened to shut down my consciousness.

Oh Wilhelmina, dearest, it was the most impressive thing you ever did.

Don't I fucking know it!

Actually, I don't think you do.

No, but… No.

I went back to my room and ran a tepid bath. To cool down. To warm up. To neutralise whatever sickness was taking hold. No bubbles. No fuss.

What did I ever do that was so impressive?

I racked my brain. Came up with no good answer.

The vampire, draped in Calanthe's velvet cloak, watched me from the bed as I kicked my clothes off and left them in a heap on the bathroom floor.

Why didn't you tell Patrick that Summer's here? It wanted to know.

'Because it doesn't matter, she won't be here very long.' I eased myself into the bathtub.

But if you'd told him, it whined, he would have come for her.

'Just shut up shut up shut up.' I dug my nails into the expansive flesh of my thighs till it hurt. Felt good.

Truth was, I wanted Patrick to stew. To experience the frustration of being left out of the loop, even though he didn't know it yet. But that made it all the sweeter.

'That's right, Wilhelmina,' Calanthe said, appearing at the bathroom door. In black cotton underwear, her skin was milky and unblemished. Perfect body with imperfect symmetry; her right arm was missing from below the elbow. Bits of tendon and tissue hung out in a gory explosion, as though that section of her arm had been ripped off. 'You're just gonna keep shtum, aren't you? You won't even tell my mum that Patrick called.' Calanthe showed no sign of being in pain. Looked as smug as ever, as though she'd reigned victorious in whatever battle she'd surrendered her arm to.

Something touched my leg, a light tapping. I looked down. Four severed fingers were floating around where my legs protruded from the water, all of them moving. I scrabbled backwards with a yelp, sending a wave coursing over the side of the bath along with two of the fingers. They squirmed and writhed on the floor tiles like giant, exotic grubs.

Calanthe laughed at my revulsion and came to the side of the bath. 'Remember when we used to take baths together?' she said, her eyes taking in my nakedness, making me feel as repugnant as her detached fingers. 'When we were little.'

I could. And they weren't fond memories. She'd often

instruct me to sit still while she tipped a jug of water over my head, hair-washing day or not. And she delighted in prodding my podgy body. You're so soft and squidgy, she delighted in telling me. As though I had a choice. I ate the same food and could run just as fast as her, but my metabolism never played fair.

I covered my chest with my arms and said, 'You're not really here.'

'Course I am, silly.' She sat on the edge of the bath. Forever sixteen, the years that had fatigued the suppleness of my skin like old knicker elastic and given me grey hairs hadn't aged her at all. She was exactly as I remembered. Immaculate white smile. Flawless skin with no pores in sight. No stretch marks or cellulite spoiling her body. The only thing wrong was her missing arm and the dark shading beneath her eyes. Could it be the vivacity of her blue irises leaking out into surrounding tissue? Spreading bruises.

Don't worry, even death can't tarnish you much, cousin.

She scooped one of her fingers out of the bath, as though handling a rare butterfly, and held it close to my face. It was blue-ish white. Wrinkled. The painted red fingernail glossy, catching the light. Blood oozed impossibly from the gored end as though somehow still wired to Calanthe's heart with an endless supply. Each drop spattered on the flabby mound of my stomach, darkening the folds and enhancing each roll of fat. I resisted the urge to retch. To cry out. The vampire fell off the bed, creating a loud clunk. Or perhaps it was the front door banging shut, reverberating through the building.

'It hurt like a bastard, you know,' Calanthe said, dropping the finger onto the shelf created by my crossed arms. Immediately it poked at the fold of my cleavage, wriggling and jabbing, taunting my breasts.

Good, I wanted to scream. But I didn't. I opened my arms and, making a sound of disgust, batted the finger with the back of my hand. Instead of sending it wide as I'd intended, it catapulted back into the water, creating a ridiculous plonk next to my right foot.

Calanthe's head tipped back, and she erupted with laughter.

Oh, how perfectly perfect she was.

'You have no intention of looking out for her, do you?' she said, her expression becoming serious in an instant. Her eyes were shrewd, even more bruised now she'd had her fun. I knew she was talking about Summer. She swivelled her hips and stepped into the bath, her feet deathly cold but real against my legs. 'You'll stay quiet and keep what you know to yourself. Because that's what you do. That's what kind of person you are. You'll let her take those drugs, and you know what?'

'What?'

'In the back of your mind, you'll hope she grows wings and wants to try them out. From the top of Whitby Abbey with any luck.'

'Don't be ridiculous.'

'So talk to her. Tell her it's a bad idea. Or tell someone else if you don't want to deal with it.'

The vampire floundered on the bedroom floor, luxurious velvet folds flapping like a dying bat's wing.

'It's none of my business what she does,' I said, petulantly.

'You made it your business when you rooted through her stuff.' Calanthe hunkered lower in the water, her back pressing against the taps, her eyes challenging me. The mangled stump of her arm dangled just above the water, which was now fully red. Opaque with her blood. 'I'd say you have a duty of care.'

'I don't have a duty of care for anyone.'

'That's you all over: me me me.' Calanthe's mouth down-turned at the sides and she pouted her bottom lip in an exaggerated display of upset. 'Just because your mother treated you like shit on her shoe and Summer like an angel doesn't make it Summer's fault.'

'I never said it was.'

'Yet there you are, steeped in bitterness.'

'That's not true. I don't even know her. Not properly.'

'Now's your chance.'

'I don't want to know her.'

'That's because she reminds you of everything you can't be.' Calanthe dropped onto her knees and leaned forward. The ceramic of the bath squeaked beneath her wet hand as she slid closer to me. And closer still. Till her cold breath touched my face and neck, scattering goosebumps across my shoulders and tightening my nipples. 'Poor Wilhelmina, you're so jealous.'

'No, I'm not.'

'Yes, you are. Just as you were of me.' She grinned. 'I should probably let you know that jealousy is way uglier than a plain face.'

'Like you'd ever know.'

'Ha.' Calanthe's knees were touching my buttocks now, her slim body imposing the space between my open legs. 'I've seen how you stare at the Scotsman in Room Two.'

'Liar.'

'Oh please. The thought of him touching you in the dark makes you all hot and bothered.' She groaned dramatically and rolled her eyes back as if in some throes of lust. When she looked at me again, she laughed at my abhorrence. 'Deep down it saddens you because you don't think someone like him could ever feel the same way about someone like you.' She poked me in the stomach with her one good forefinger. The soft doughy flesh ate it up. 'I mean, ugh.' She shuddered. 'You're like a tired old hippopotamus, look at you. No one in their right mind would fuck you, let alone fall in love and marry and live happily ever after with you.'

This particular shot of venom hurt most. Tears stung my

eyes.

Calanthe's burned with pure antagonism. 'Summer, on the other hand,' she said, biting her bottom lip with her top teeth, 'I bet she'd turn the Scotsman's head.'

If Calanthe wasn't already dead, I thought in that moment I might strangle her. 'Shut up.'

She laughed that kitteny laugh of hers and patted the side of my face, a gesture intended to further provoke my rage. 'Oh yes, I bet he'd love to bang her.'

My jaw tightened.

'But you?' She stood up. Bloodied water washed down her legs in pink rivulets. 'I bet he wouldn't even touch you with his camera's flash.' She stepped out of the bath, a gored goddess.

You'd look good on my walls.

Just shut up. Shut up. SHUT UP!

At the door, Calanthe waved her stump at me, and from it cherry blossom bloomed. Then she disappeared, like a message that hadn't been properly delivered. But one that stirred my subconscious.

Uh, the vampire said before blacking out.

Then I think I did too.

15

Catherine Hall

2003

'Where are you going?' I'd put on some black jeans and a plain black t-shirt and back-combed my hair at the roots, hoping Calanthe was in a good mood and would let me go out with her. It was Goth Weekend, so the whole town was buzzing. I'd been out earlier, just after breakfast, to survey the atmosphere, venturing only as far as the whale bones where I was afforded a view across the harbour; a vast area of bustling blackness. I'd sat on the grass, listening to The Sisters of Mercy on my iPod, feeling some strange kinship with the abbey in the distance. Surrounded by people, but desperately lonely. Throngs of goths passed by, most of them in black lace, velvet, satin or PVC – or various combinations of all. Most items of clothing were buckled or laced or zipped tightly into place. Never too early in the day for a spot of seducing whatever onlookers happened to look. I imagined the *Demeter* might be docked in the harbour just out of sight. That the Count might be out there searching the crowds for his Elisabeta. Climbing the famous steps. One-hundred and ninety-nine. Then back down to start again. However many times it might take.

I'd gone back to The Zoltan. Found Calanthe checking her reflection in the full-length mirror on her bedroom wall. She was wearing her velvet cloak over a black minidress. Had put on false eyelashes and black lipstick. Looked like a Disney princess, all doe eyed and alluring, but deadly and vampire-like. We were both sixteen, but she looked twenty.

'None of your business,' she said in answer to my question.

It was very rare that Calanthe wanted to hang around with me anymore, especially not when her older friends were there. I cramped her style. Gave away her true age because I looked every bit the gawky sixteen-year-old. Spotty-faced with braces straightening my crooked teeth and puppy fat (so Aunt Lyrica insisted) still sticking to whatever curves might have tried to form beneath.

'Can't I come with you today?'

'Definitely not.' Calanthe prised her gaze away from herself to give me a stern glare. 'Look at you, you're such a frump.' She laughed, a spiteful sound that stabbed at the spaces between my well insulated ribs like hungry birds' pecking beaks. 'And look at your teeth, all that metal. Makes you look about twelve. I'm beginning to think Tom Dockin is your dad.'

'You're such a bitch.'

She shrugged. 'Tough love. It's for your own good.'

'You won't let me come because you're going to see *him* again, aren't you?' I said.

'Who?'

'Arthur Holmwood.' Calanthe was seeing some local bloke in his thirties who had a wife and two kids, a silver BMW and gold Rolex. He bought Calanthe expensive perfume and took her for 'long drives' when he was supposed to be working late. She'd nicknamed him Arthur Holmwood after the character in Bram Stoker's *Dracula*. One of Lucy Westenra's suitors. I never knew his real name. And I'm guessing he never knew her real age.

'Don't be daft,' she said, rolling her eyes. 'It's

Goth Weekend. He's much too sensible and straight-laced.'

'Quincey Morris then?' He was a local bricklayer, around twenty-five with a tattooed neck and brooding temperament. Again, nicknamed after another of Lucy Westenra's admirers. Not because he was anything like Morris – for the record, neither was Arthur Holmwood anything like his namesake – but because Calanthe didn't want to use their real names. Might be too damaging to all concerned if her real age ever got out.

'God no, he's much too bigoted to appreciate the goth scene,' she said.

But apparently he was good with his tongue.

I was yet to even kiss a boy. Or girl. I didn't suppose I'd mind either way, I thought, as long it was someone I could connect with emotionally and intelligently. And someone who wouldn't mind my braces. Calanthe loved men. Straight up. There was never any question about that. She was a slut, a liar, a thief and a recreational drug user. Aunt Lyrica had no clue, she was too busy running The Zoltan single-handedly.

Calanthe left the room and I followed.

'So where are you going?' I insisted.

'Anywhere where you aren't there.'

I scowled at her for a moment, then watched as the front door opened and a man stepped into the foyer. Calanthe and I fell still and stared. Awestruck. In a grey suit and matching top hat, the man had long dark hair and the same sort of blue lensed sunglasses worn by Gary Oldman in the 1992 *Bram Stoker's Dracula* film covered his eyes. He even had the same moustache and tiny wisp of beard as Prince Vlad.

My heart soared. He was beautiful.

'Can I help?' Calanthe said, coming unstuck from the momentary blip of delighted surprise that had rendered her motionless. She sauntered over to the man like a lucky black cat.

He knocked his glasses down the bridge of his nose with a gloved finger and took in the sight of her, his unveiled eyes alight with quiet, unapologetic desire. 'Left my wallet in my room,' he said, pointing to the stairs.

Calanthe's smile widened. 'Oh, you're staying here?'

'Room Three.' The man winked.

She stood to one side and wafted her arm toward the stairs, as if granting him access because she was queen of everything. He tipped his top hat and grinned a wolfish grin. Completely ignored me. Then made his way upstairs.

Calanthe turned to me and, temporarily forgetting her sense of cool, fanned her face with her hand and mouthed *Dracula's staying here!*

I eyed the stairs, now empty. My insides excitably stirred. 'I know.'

'Anyway,' Calanthe said, resuming her prior standoffish mode and waving a dismissive hand at me. 'See you later, Wilhelmina. Don't follow me. I'll know.'

I thought about doing exactly that, just to spite her, but decided not to. It wasn't worth the risk. If I pissed her off enough, she'd concoct a story to persuade Aunt Lyrica to make me go home. And since my mother was on the verge of giving birth to a 'much wanted' child, I'd be even more invisible there.

I sat on the wall outside and watched people coming and going. I wished I could be part of someone's group, so I might belong. After a few minutes had passed, Dracula from Room Three came out of The Zoltan. He breezed past me without looking and headed towards North Terrace. When he was halfway down the street, I jumped off the wall. Decided I'd follow him. Andrew Eldritch's voice pumped through my earphones singing about dominion and prayers and lending me a slight swagger. Certainly more boldness than if I'd had to listen to my thoughts with nothing but mundane street sounds to back them up. I kept a safe distance, far enough for him not to realise I was trailing him, but not too far that I'd lose him. In my head I was Van Helsing. A noble vampire slayer, my pockets filled with vials of holy water, wooden stakes and silver crucifixes. I was chasing the monster to his lair.

Beyond the fantasy, I needed to know what a man like him did for pleasure. What made him tick. Was his getup a weekend costume only? Did he wear jeans and t-shirts during the week like everyone else? And if so, did he command such attention in ordinary clothes? Or was he Prince Vlad at all times? My head swam with the sheer exhilaration of imagined scenarios. None of them plausible. Not in the slightest. He led me to Pier Road, towards the amusement arcades, and I saw how everyone else noticed him along the way, especially the women. His presence was a magnet. A glorious lure. He dipped into Funland Amusements and was instantly swallowed by the flock of people using its slot machines and video games — mostly grown goths, but lots of regular kids too.

I hurried inside, nudging my way through the crowd and standing on my tiptoes, trying to spot his top hat. But he was gone. Devoured. Bright, flashing lights and the sound of jingles, buzzers, bells and the metallic jangle of loose change being dispensed surrounded me. All of it visually and audibly loud. My heart raced.

Where are you?

A recorded voice at the donkey derby stall, which spanned most of the wall to the left, announced: And they're off! I dashed along several rows of two-pence machines, searching. Frantic now. Breathing hard. Towards the back of the arcade was a range of zombie video games and motorbike simulators. It was darker, more adult, and there were fewer players here. Still no Dracula.

See me, I thought. See me now.

I whirled round to retrace my steps, and there he was. Right in front of me. So close I could smell the musk of his cologne and the faint embedded cigarette smoke on his clothes. I gargled a yelp in my throat and stepped backwards. All the holy water and other defences in my pockets vanished. Disintegrated. I wasn't a slayer. Not of this beast.

He stepped closer, forcing me further back till I was against the wall. He put his arm out, penning me in, and stooped to my level so his face was right in mine.

'You're following me,' he said.

I shook my head, ready to lie. Part of my brain daring to imagine that under different circumstances, if I was someone else, this is the position he might adopt if he was about to kiss me.

'Don't,' he said, as if to stop my thoughts before they spiralled out of control. 'You should be careful, kid. You don't know what monsters are out and about.'

'Monsters?' I exhaled a snort of laughter through my nose and squared my shoulders with some element of false bravado. 'I know all about monsters.'

'Yeah?' His eyebrows rose above his glasses in what I expected was humour.

'Yeah. And there's none worse than Tom Dockin.'

'Who's he?'

'The bogeyman.'

I expected Dracula might laugh, but he didn't. He merely knocked his glasses down his nose and fixed me with his steely blue gaze. 'It's not the bogeyman you should fear,' he said. 'There's worse evil amongst the living.' He winked at me and I felt his breath on my face like the most tender of kisses. Then he turned and walked away.

16

Catherine Hall

2019

Aunt Lyrica and Summer came back from the supermarket laden with shopping bags. I met them in the hallway, the ends of my hair still wet from lying in the bath with Calanthe and her severed fingers and all of her blood, and insisted I'd carry some stuff through to the kitchen.

'Oh, you're coming to help now?' Aunt Lyrica said teasingly, as I relieved her of two bags and took one from Summer. 'Bit bloody late.' When I didn't respond, she asked, 'How are you feeling, anyway?'

The truth was, I was sick with nostalgia; the promised ugliness of the past I'd suppressed and couldn't yet see. And woozy and spent with circumspection, the way The Zoltan channelled through me like I was a device and its ghosts were using me, scrolling through my thoughts to find the answers they wanted and the ones I didn't. But I told her, 'Okay.'

'That's good to hear.'

I passed the door to the dining room and out the corner of my eye glimpsed the canvas on the chimneybreast wall. A brooding figure skulked there on the fabric in thick black acrylic strokes. Its (his) mouth wide, bearing silver teeth that were too shiny. I stopped and backtracked. Summer walked into me.

'What's up?' she said, clicking her tongue with mild impatience.

I turned my head to look at the canvas. Saw the crimson rose and its shadow.

'Nothing,' I said. 'Thought I saw something.'

'What?'

'Doesn't matter.'

'Well hurry up,' Aunt Lyrica called from the end of the convoy. 'My bloody arms are dropping off.'

We unpacked the bags in the kitchen together and I noted how Aunt Lyrica and Summer seemed to have made up for a lot of the lost time that divided them. Their rapport was easy, their chatter effortless. Amazing what a couple of hours at the supermarket can do.

'Check out what Aunt Lyrica bought for me,' Summer said, pulling an oval link chain from beneath the neckline of her top and showing me the pendant that was affixed. A silver rose inset with Whitby jet.

'Nice,' I said, nodding. Though I didn't think it was very fitting that she should have it. I was the black rose. The shadow. I smiled nonetheless, but it felt too much like a snarl that I couldn't contain. Summer didn't seem to notice. Or if she did, she wasn't bothered.

'I got something for you too,' Aunt Lyrica said, pulling a boxed cake from one of the carrier bags. 'Chocolate fudge, your favourite.'

'Wow, thanks.' I tried to look grateful, was definitely less snarly, but was suddenly self-conscious about the weight around my midriff and how the cake would contribute to that. Calanthe's finger was still buried in my rolls of fat. I could feel it there. Pinching. Prodding. 'A whole cake, just for me?'

Aunt Lyrica winked. 'We'll help you eat it.'

Not just for me then.

Summer giggled, already moving on. 'That man behind us in the checkout queue, did you see his face when he overheard us talking about walking back here with all these bags?'

Aunt Lyrica grinned. 'Yeah, too many people these days think a bit of physical exertion might kill them.' She didn't look at me when she said this, but Calanthe's finger dug deeper and harder. My waistband constricted.

I stood up straight. Breathed in.

'He didn't offer to give us a lift though, did he?' Summer said.

'To be honest, I'm pleased he didn't.' Aunt Lyrica laughed. 'He stunk of TCP.'

'Uh, yeah.' Summer pretended to retch.

'I could have picked you up if you'd called,' I said, not sure why. What difference did it make now?

'Here, could you put this in the fridge, please?' Aunt Lyrica passed a four-pint carton of milk to Summer, as though I hadn't spoken at all.

Summer reached for it. 'Yeah, course.'

Would either of them notice if I wasn't here? I wondered. If I was to leave would they really care?

'Listen,' Aunt Lyrica said, 'I was thinking, since all three of us are here together, how about I treat us all to a meal this evening? There's an Italian restaurant I think you'll both love.'

Summer nodded, but I was overcome with dread. It sluiced over me like pond water, slimy and cold.

'I dunno,' I said, my voice sounding strained because my throat was suddenly too narrow for the excuses that were trying to rise to my tongue. My skin began to curl beneath the surface in retaliation for the obligation I might yet fulfil. I scratched at my arms. No. 'I think I'll give it a miss, actually. I've still got a headache. It's lingering. You know?' Truth was, I couldn't bear the thought of sitting like a sad sack while they chatted and laughed together all evening. The newly formed bond between them was clear, they'd taken to each other so fluently.

Aunt Lyrica could pretend she had Calanthe back and Summer could pretend she had Mother back. I didn't fit into that equation. I'd be the barely noticed, yet expected, silence between the build-up of a joke and the delivery of the punchline, the joke entirely on me. 'Think I'll have an early night, try to shake it off. Hopefully I'll be better tomorrow.'

Aunt Lyrica flashed me a look that I wasn't able to decipher with any amount of confidence, but it seemed sullen and suspicious and I assumed its overall message was: Thanks for ruining that idea.

'You two go ahead though,' I said, trying to smooth the situation while appearing put out. I clutched my head for added effect. 'I'm sure you'll have fun without me.'

Won't you ever.

Aunt Lyrica looked to Summer for her input.

She was no less enthused. 'I'm still up for it.'

'Okay, I'll book us a table.'

'Right then,' I said. 'I'm going for a lie down.'

Aunt Lyrica nodded and Summer ignored me.

I skulked upstairs to my room and began rearranging stuff. I moved the wastepaper basket to the opposite side of the room, nudged the bed closer to the window, put my work diary on top of the wardrobe, swapped the bottom drawer with the top drawer in the bedside cabinet and lined six church candles along the edge of the bath. I thought if I changed all this, I might change other stuff too. But it didn't feel right. Made me too anxious. So I put everything back as it was, then did twenty laps of the room, from the door to the window, touching the surface of the dresser each time I passed. Eventually I lay on the bed next to the vampire and fell asleep. When I awoke, I heard voices downstairs.

Aunt Lyrica and Summer were in the hallway, ready to go out. Summer had borrowed some of Aunt Lyrica's clothes: black lacy top and leather-look leggings. She was much too grown-up. Much too Calanthe. Aunt Lyrica's patchouli fragrance was especially strong. Reminded me of childhood. I ran a hand through my bedraggled hair and told whoever wanted to hear it, 'You look great.'

'Oh, hey.' Aunt Lyrica was checking her lipstick in the mirror by the door. 'Are you sure you don't want to come?'

'Next time, definitely.' Though somehow I knew there wouldn't be a next time.

'You do seem a bit peaky,' Aunt Lyrica said, moving away from the mirror to examine me at closer range. 'Your eyes, they're a bit... I dunno. Maybe you *should* have an early night.'

Before I made another empty promise, the front door opened and Dan Munro stepped inside with a blast of cold air. He seemed surprised (perhaps even scared) to find the three of us in the hallway. As though we'd been purposefully waiting for him. An ambush of sorts.

'Hi,' Aunt Lyrica said. 'How was your day?'

'Er, yeah, not bad.' He closed the door behind him and stood on the doormat, afraid to move. 'You off out?'

'Yeah, taking my niece to Portofino's.'

His attention drifted to Summer, and he nodded.

I bet he'd love to bang her.

He smiled widely, his eyes sparking. 'Well, enjoy.'

'Thanks,' Summer said. 'I will.'

Dan pardoned himself then and headed towards the stairs. He didn't look at me once. I wasn't even a shadow, I realised. I was the shadow of a shadow lurking in the dismal space of pointlessness. Upstairs, the vampire wept softly.

'See you later, Cat,' Aunt Lyrica called as she and Summer left.

Silence ensued after the door banged shut, marking Dan's presence in The Zoltan as something enormous. I stood for a moment, unable to move, unsure what to do.

Then I heard a movement in the dining room.

I found Calanthe sitting at Dan's breakfast table in the window, basking in the orange glow of the streetlight outside. The stump of her missing arm bled onto the white tablecloth, and a revolting wet sucking sound made my innards clench. As I drew closer, I saw a mass of small, glistening bodies squirming in the tarry pool of her blood. An assortment of insects and worms. Bathing, drinking or drowning.

'Poor Wilhelmina,' Calanthe said, tilting her face further into the light, showing me that a huge chunk of her cheek was missing. Appeared to have been bitten off. Through the jagged hole, her teeth were small bones nestled in a line of healthy gum. 'So unlucky in love.'

'You weren't exactly lucky yourself,' I told her, unable to stop gawping at this monstrous thing she'd become.

Calanthe laughed. As she did, the side of her tongue protruded from the gory gap in her cheek. She put her hand to her mouth as if to hide it. 'True enough, I'll give you that.' She sat forward, her eyes gleaming. The powdery orange from the streetlight made her glow with ethereal decadence. Bugs spilled to the floor. 'You've always felt like you're in the dark.'

'Because everyone always made me feel that way.'

'There are monsters in the dark, aren't there?'

'You should know.'

'Oh, I do. Believe me, I do.' Calanthe curled some of her matted hair round her fingers, then stamped her foot. 'For crying out loud, Wilhelmina, why don't you just knock on his door?'

'Whose?'

She rolled her eyes, looking peevish. 'Don't act the fool, you know who I mean.'

The darkness of the room breathed down my neck with dirty big inhalations and exhalations. Sticking to my skin like someone else's sweat.

Snip snip snip.

There was a thud upstairs. Dan's door closing. Then footsteps on the stairs.

'Too late.' Calanthe huffed. 'Missed your chance. He's off out now.'

'Good for him.'

One corner of her mouth rose in the smallest of smirks. 'You realise where he's going though, don't you?'

'Where?'

'Oh, come on, you noticed the way he looked at Summer. Mum practically gave him an invitation.'

Taking my niece to Portofino's.

'Portofino's?'

'You're appallingly slow on the uptake, Wilhelmina.' Calanthe groaned and reached out to grab my arm, but I shrugged away and ran into the hallway just in time to see Dan leaving The Zoltan. Only, for a split second it wasn't Dan. It was Dracula from Room Three.

You should be careful, kid. You don't know what monsters are out and about.

I raced upstairs and grabbed Calanthe's velvet cloak from my bed, scattering the vampire to the floor. It barely protested. As I fastened the cloak about my throat and pulled its hood over my head, I thundered back down the stairs. Calanthe watched from the dining room doorway, a trail of blood behind her on the floor. Insects swarmed on the doorframe.

'You know what happened to me, Wilhelmina,' she said, scowling. 'You always fucking knew.'

I ignored her and hurtled into the street, glimpsing Dracula who was Dan again as he disappeared round the bend in Crescent Avenue. I ran after him, seductive black velvet flapping all around me like wings, flirting with the night.

It's not the bogeyman you should fear. There's worse evil among the living.

Let's find out.

17

Catherine Hall

2019

Dan's pace quickened. I wondered if he realised I was following him.

Did I really think he was heading to Portofino's?

Not really.

I was sixteen again, following Dracula, and I was thirty-two, following a perfect stranger. The similarities were striking, yet the two occasions were not at all alike. The same dangerous excitement filled my heart though, that much was true. Dan was the second man to have piqued my interest so much I'd given chase. Only this time I didn't know why I was so entranced. I decided I'd follow him wherever he went, if that's what it took to find out. He passed under the whale bone arch, shoulders hunched and head bowed to the wind, and headed down the steps to Khyber Pass. As I descended the steps, perversely indifferent to being spotted, he turned at the bottom.

I was close. So close.

To what?

You know what happened to me, Wilhelmina.

I couldn't see it with my eyes, but the North Sea – so vast, so full, yet so lonely – bristled away from the very shore upon which the *Demeter* was yet to land. It called to me with its shush-hush voice: I long, I long, I long. And its salty sorrow was subtle on my face and lips, having been swept towards the West Cliff by the uncaring wind. It made me want to weep. Beyond the captive stretch of sea on which many fishing boats bobbed, the abbey shivered in the moonlessness. Waiting, always waiting.

There was a smattering of people out and about, but I doubted any of them had noticed me. Clouds filled the sky. It was darkly dark. I was invisible. The cold penetrated Calanthe's cloak and my ugly clothes beneath, but I didn't care. Was too caught up in the chase. On Pier Road Dan kept walking past the amusement arcades on the right.

Heading towards Portofino's?

Surely not.

At the end of the row, he crossed the road and stopped at the metal railings to gaze out at the harbour, across to the silhouette of St Mary's which skulked like a long-abandoned chrysalis. Gulls swooped in the bleak underbelly of the sky, their outlines ghostly. I imagined their eyes were Dan's and was suddenly convinced that whatever they saw they transmitted the information to him. She's there, right there! She's following you!

I ducked out of view, hiding behind a white wooden stall that had sold fortunes for as long as I could remember. A staple souvenir from a trip to the seaside. When we were around fifteen, Calanthe and I had gone inside and the owner, a self-proclaimed descendant of Gypsy Rose Lee, had taken money from us and told Calanthe she was destined for great things: a successful career, a handsome husband, three bright kids and a second home in the south of France. Afterwards the woman told me I'd do well for myself too: a secure job and a steady income. As with everything else, my fate was flatter and duller than Calanthe's, lacking any and all enticing details. The clairvoyant said she could see a man in my life, but he was little more than a shadow over my shoulder. Too obscure for her to define. Or maybe I was standing behind him and he was much too close and she couldn't focus on him and actually I was his shadow. Either way, we were bound together. And that had been that. She ushered me and Calanthe back outside into the breezy, sunshiny day.

I wondered now, if she'd looked hard enough, would the clairvoyant have seen a glint of metal at the man's mouth. I also wondered if Calanthe rattled around in some house in the South of France, her fingers in a jewellery box and her arm wrapped in velvet, stored in a treasure chest.

Dan moved off, walking much more slowly this time. Contemplating? Feeling indecisive? Playing with me? He glanced up at the sign for The Dracula Experience – a walk-through amusement attraction, much like a ghost-train but without the train – and came to a stop again. After what seemed to be a self-deprecating shake of the head, he grinned to himself and stepped into the foyer.

Wrapping my arms around myself and shivering against the cold, I watched from outside as he spoke to a young woman behind the counter. Then once he'd disappeared from view, I lurched inside. The foyer was brightly lit. Warm. Blood seeped back to my face. That or my cheeks were melting, sliding down to create jowls that would reach my shoulders. I imagined I looked like roadkill swathed in velvet. The young woman behind the counter flicked through the pages of a glossy magazine, cracked chewing gum between her teeth, and barely looked up. 'Evening,' she said. 'Just the one?'

'Yeah.' I pulled out a fiver and after pocketing my change and admission ticket, stepped through a sliding door into the building's dark lair without being instructed to do so. I'd been inside many times before. With and without Calanthe. 'I know what to do,' I said.

At first my eyes were blind, and speakers crackled overhead: the distant cry of a lone, hungry wolf in dark mountains, wind ripping through castle windows and haunted trees, the drip-drap-drip of water leaking into an empty cellar or dungeon room. I was in all of these places at once, and yet none. I couldn't be, I realised, because I was in a never-ending tunnel with Tom Dockin. Just ahead, his broad shouldered, statuesque presence made the darkness shiver away nervously. He jolted my senses. And I realised he was the purpose of this homecoming.

Laughter erupted from the speakers.

'Oh, Wilhelmina,' Calanthe chided. She'd followed me here to taunt me more.

A flare of white light filled the corridor, blinding me to darkness again. I expected Calanthe might touch me, that she'd slide the cold, wet stump of her arm across my skin, just for laughs, using my temporary handicap to her advantage. To delight in my repulsion. But nothing touched me.

Breathe in. Breathe out. Breathe in, breathe in. Breathe out.

My heart hammered and the swirling, pulsing shapes behind my retinas gradually faded. When my eyes adjusted once again to the gloom, I saw that the hulking figure of Tom Dockin had moved closer. The reek of his farmyard musk was undeniable, and the ratchety grating of his metal teeth loud.

Snip snip snip.

'It's not the bogeyman you should fear,' Dracula from Room Three said, his voice a retro-crackle over the speakers. 'There's worse evil among the living.'

But the bogeyman was right there in front of me, and I didn't think there could be anything as frightening as that. Nothing ever. Never. No.

'Wilhelmina, here.' I spun round and found Calanthe behind me, in a white satin slip, the likes of which I'd never seen her in before. Blood spoiled the slinky fabric to great symbolic effect, though what the symbolism was

I didn't know. Both of her arms were missing from the elbow down. She grinned at me from her ruined face. 'You remember that day, don't you?' she said.

'What day?'

'Hey, kid, you should be careful,' Dracula from Room Three said. He was right behind me. The smell of his cologne and cigarette breath stirred old memories. Old feelings. Old want. 'You don't know what monsters are out and about.'

I turned sideways and flattened my back against the wall, like a frightened animal. Calanthe was blocking the way to the right, and Dracula from Room Three was looming to the left. He grinned, baring sharp incisors which he hadn't had before.

'Tom Dockin's behind you,' I warned.

Snip snip snip.

'The bogeyman?' Dracula from Room Three laughed in disdain. 'He's behind us all if we'd only care to look.' He snatched out, gripping my wrist with bone-bruising force, and pulled me to him. Inflated thoughts crowded my head. Many that didn't matter, and some that did, but there was no room to understand any of them. I felt dizzy. Weak. Could scarcely breathe. I inhaled just enough to know that Dracula smelt of dust and candles and incense. Of churches, too. I wanted to melt into the darkness. Into him. To cease to exist, except in this moment.

White light flashed again, lighting up the entire corridor in intermittent bursts. Dracula's eyes glowed red behind blue lenses. He held me tightly against his chest, an alabaster statue breathing life. Too harsh and too painful to be anything but dangerous.

'You'd look good on my walls,' he said, the words warm and sticky against my forehead.

Calanthe giggled. 'Not as good as me.' She did a pirouette, the gory stumps of her arms held upright. 'I'm a rose, she's a wallflower.'

Dracula put his fingers beneath my chin, angling my face towards his.

I long. I long. I long.

I closed my eyes and waited (prayed) for his cold mouth to reach mine.

'Excuse me! Hello?'

Startled, I turned and saw the woman from the foyer squinting into the darkness, shining a torch along the passage.

'Is everything all right?'

Her words meant nothing, and I thought she might as well be talking in an alien language, but my mouth moved and I heard myself say, 'Yeah.' I staggered backwards and saw that Dracula had frozen. His skin was wax. Real wax. Always had been. He didn't even look like him anymore. And Calanthe was nowhere. Neither was Tom Dockin. I could smell goat's hair at the back of my nose, and the smell coated my tongue. Everything I had and hadn't thought to eat that day heaved in my guts. I needed fresh air.

Another flash of white lightning got me moving. Blind and panicky, I fled down the corridor, away from the woman and the wax model and the hallucinations in my wake. I had to find the exit to purge my lungs. I rounded a corner, gripping the wall, and saw Dan up ahead.

'You're following me,' he said. His stance was cool. Unperturbed. He pretended to read a plaque on the wall.

'I'm not.'

'You're also a terrible liar.'

'Okay. Maybe I am.'

'So why?' Dan turned from the plaque, gave me his full attention.

'You remind me of someone.'

'Who?'

'Dracula.'

Dan snorted. 'Why on earth do I remind you of

Dracula?'

'Not *the* Dracula,' I said. 'That would be silly.' Or would it? 'Dracula from Room Three.'

'Who's he?'

'A man I once met.'

'Ah.' Dan nodded. Rubbed his chin. 'Do I look like him?'

'No, not at all.'

His hand flopped to his side. 'Then I don't understand.'

I shrugged. Neither did I. Like a river follows its course to the sea, my need to follow Dan was automatic. Beyond the realms of my conscious understanding.

'What is it you want?' he asked.

This question was loaded with too much ambiguity, yet offered possibilities at a magnitude I could hardly bear. There was so much I could say. So much I could…

White lights strobed above us. Quick bursts like a camera's flash.

And then, just like that, I knew. Like the clearing of fog, things became clearer.

'Your camera,' I said, lurching forward and grasping his arm.

Dan tilted his head to one side, his expression one of surprise. 'You want my camera?'

'No. *He* had one too, that's why I thought I knew you. But it was your camera all along, it reminded me of him and his camera and all the things I didn't want to be reminded of.'

'Dracula from Room Three had a camera?'

'Yes.' That day, that fateful day, he'd taken pictures. He'd done things. Things I'd wanted to forget.

You know what happened to me, Wilhelmina.

Dan shook his head. 'That still doesn't explain…'

'You'd look good on my walls!' I said, exhilarated with the recollection but terrified by all it might mean and what might come after.

'Excuse me?'
Come with me.
Dan faded away and my subconscious opened up.

18

Catherine Hall

2003

I walked the streets like a stray for hours, immersing myself in the goth culture and marvelling at the level of acceptance the locals presented when their town had been sprung upon by such morbid flamboyance. All around me were trad goths, cyber goths, New Romantics, cosplayers, steampunks, posers, crossovers of all the above – so many subcultures sharing Whitby's thoroughfares. All of them in love with the vampire fable Bram Stoker had put in place. A feel-good vibe emanated from the core of the fishing town, making every part animated and vibrant, despite there being so much black. I smiled now and then, finding myself caught up in a feeling of togetherness for brief snatches at a time. But the fact remained, despite my attempt at wearing black clothes to fit in, I was alone. Still not fitting in. A fly flailing on the surface of an exotic, punchy elixir that I wanted to drink, not drown in. And all the while, I couldn't get Dracula from Room Three out of my head. He'd utterly seduced my thoughts with his Oldman style.

It's not the bogeyman you should fear, he'd warned. There's worse evil amongst the living. But was it a general warning? A flippant but thoughtful piece of advice in case I followed the wrong person one day. Or was it more of a personal warning? A cautionary threat to ensure I stopped following him. There'd been something wolfish about his glare, after all. Not an absolute deterrent by any means. It had served only to fuel my curiosity. And had I possessed the same confidence as Calanthe, I've no doubt I'd have continued to follow him.

Eventually, when morning had been chewed up and partially digested by a provocative afternoon, and the wind had a cruel nip because it wound itself round all the shaded areas the sun could no longer reach, I went back to The Zoltan to see if I'd feel less lonely not surrounded by others. When I got there, a persistent drone filled the entire building. Aunt Lyrica was vacuuming. I fled down the hallway to Calanthe's room, hoping to go unseen in case I got roped into helping with chores. Usually I wouldn't have minded, but the fiction of romance filled my head and I wanted to be alone with my thoughts. To shape and sort them. To dream I was Mina Murray.

Calanthe wasn't in her room, for which I was grateful. I hadn't expected her to be. Her curfew was ten o'clock on weekend evenings, so during Goth Weekend I knew she'd milk that to the last second, probably beyond. When no constructive sorting of my thoughts had happened within five minutes, I flopped on my back on Calanthe's bed with an Anne Rice book. *The Vampire Lestat.* But I soon found that reading was a pointless exercise. I kept going over the opening paragraph again and again, my mind returning to Dracula, Room Three.

Room Three: with the painting of sunset-orange wallflowers on the landing wall outside. The painting of sunset-orange wallflowers: concealing a hole in the plaster. A hole in the plaster: camouflaged on the inside by dark swirling patterns on the wallpaper. Nobody had noticed this aggravated minor disrepair, except Calanthe. She'd shown it to me years ago, after she'd made the miniscule hole larger. Aside from being a thief, Calanthe was a snoop, always watching people. Not only stealing their belongings, but their privacy too. Calanthe knew all the nooks and crannies within The Zoltan. Every creaking board and door hinge. She knew about all the spyholes, whether their being there was deliberate or happenstance.

The things some people get up to when they think no one's watching, she'd once told me. You wouldn't believe.

Well, you shouldn't be watching, I'd said.

You're such a frump, Wilhelmina.

Well, we'll see about that. I jumped to my feet, determined to prove her wrong. I pulled open the bedroom door and listened intently. The steady hum of the vacuum cleaner had stopped, and in its place the muffled sound of voices on television travelled down the hallway. Aunt Lyrica must be having a tea break. I crept to the lounge, peering through the gap of the open door. Aunt Lyrica was on the couch, a cup of tea in her hand, watching some old rerun of *Murder, She Wrote*. Jessica Fletcher was chatting to some handsome but tragically retro-looking man and making sleuthing look like a glamorous profession and flirting as easy as brushing your teeth. Calanthe would make a good detective, I thought. Only not as amiable as Ms Fletcher. After dodging past the lounge without being seen, I raced upstairs, trying to be as light on my feet as possible. On the landing I stood for a moment to catch my breath, guilty but excited about what I was about to do.

Don't do it.

Just do it.

Don't do it.

Just do it.

I knitted my fingers together. Bit my bottom lip. Edged towards Room Three. Eyed the door as though something dangerous lurked on the other side of it. And maybe it did. The molten-orange of the wallflower petals in the painting were as heated as my shame as I gripped the edges of the picture frame and prised it away from the wall, slipping it off its metal hook.

I'm not doing anything wrong, I reminded myself. Dracula will be out there among the crowds of Whitby being beautiful. All I'll see is the unoccupied room with his stuff in it.

So what's the point?

To prove Calanthe wrong. I'm not a frump. I can be daring and spontaneous too. I can be…

'I love your body. Your skin.' Dracula's gruff voice came from beyond the wall to Room Three.

I froze.

He's in there he's in there he's in there.

A kitteny laugh followed.

Calanthe?

My fingers furled and unfurled around the frame of the wallflower painting.

'It feels like fresh roses,' Dracula concluded.

My blood fizzed with red rage, black jealousy and all the greyness in between. I put my right eye to the hole in the wall to peep inside Room Three. Dracula stalked around the bed, an SLR camera in his hands, his eye at the viewfinder.

Snap. Flash. Snap. Flash.

He was shirtless, his skin white and smooth. His torso lean. On the bed, completely naked, Calanthe posed. Her perfect form was laid out for him to ogle. He climbed onto the mattress with feline grace and knelt beside her, his hair splaying down his back in glossy black tresses. He lowered the camera from his face and stooped to kiss her. Calanthe accepted his mouth with hers, and didn't object to his explorative free hand, which caressed her right breast, thumbing her nipple, making it hard.

'Can I see you again?' he said.

'Maybe.'

He made an appreciative growl in his throat, his eyes sparking dangerously, boring into hers with something that seemed aggressive, but not. Something that made my insides turn inside out. 'You're like a goddess,' he said.

Calanthe refused to look away. Didn't even blink. 'I know.'

'You'd look good on my walls.' He was breathing more heavily now.

'Mmm hmm.' She was relaxed. In control.

'I could spend hours looking at you.'

Calanthe propped herself up on her elbows, seemingly amused. 'Could you afford to?'

'I don't live life with restrictions,' he told her. 'Monetary or otherwise.'

'Oh?' She smiled, her eyes alight with curiosity. 'What makes you so special?'

He gripped her breast more firmly in his hand, a gesture that made her yelp and me feel funny all over. 'I just always get what I want. Always have done.'

'Then we're not unalike.'

He nodded. Victorious. 'Shall I ask you again?'

'If you must.'

'Come with me.' It wasn't a question so much as a hopeful command.

'I'll think about it.'

'Okay. Will this help?' He lowered his face and took her nipple between his teeth, his hands busy with the fastener of his trousers.

Calanthe turned her head, looked at me and grinned.

She'd known I was there all along!

This realisation pricked the underside of my face with a revulsion so strong bile soured my windpipe. The wallflowers roared with such flaming heat in my hands, I almost dropped the painting.

How could we possibly interact after this?

How I could look her in the eye without recalling the minutiae of the unfolding intimacy I'd borne witness to. The blush-pink of her nipple squeezed between Dracula's thumb and forefinger. The tidy space between her legs. The knowledge that their encounter had in some small way, on her part at least, been played out for my benefit. But mostly the self-recrimination that I could have looked away at any time. But I'd chosen not to. And she knew that.

She knew that!

I wanted to die.

With trembling fingers, I rehung the painting. It took three attempts, and the mattress springs beyond the wallflowers had begun to creak. Slowly at first, then unfettered and hard. The sound of my lungs struggling for air. I ran downstairs with the sickly knowledge that things would never be the same. How could they be? My skull pounded with a black headache blooming red. My skin beneath my clothes felt like dead rose petals turned to mulch.

Why her? Why did everything good always happen to her?

I needed to get out. To go to…

'Oh, Cat, there you are.' Aunt Lyrica appeared in the hallway holding her mug. 'I have some good news.'

I bristled, immediately sensing it would be nothing of the sort.

'Your mum called,' she said. 'You have a baby sister. Born first thing this morning.'

'Oh.' My heart plummeted. Crashed to the cankerous pit of my stomach.

'Seven pounds three ounces. They've named her Summer. Maybe you should call…'

I turned and bolted from The Zoltan, fleeing down Crescent Avenue, knowing that I'd go to the grounds of St Mary's to be among its old gravestones and their dead. Because at that point, I thought, I may as well be too.

19

Catherine Hall

2019

'Cat?' Dan gripped my arms. Held me upright. His nearness was oppressive in the narrow corridor. His eyes too spectral in the gloom. Too blue. 'Are you okay?'

I shook my head.

'What happened?' he said.

'I didn't want to remember.'

'Remember what?'

I shrugged away from him, stumbling backwards, catching my elbow on the wall. I glared at him as if it was all his fault. If I hadn't seen him standing in the foyer of The Zoltan two days ago holding his camera, all this wouldn't be happening. I'd be imperturbably unaware. Bad memories would be still shackled in some obscure, defunct part of my brain. Starved of acknowledgement and the damning ownership of self-blame.

'I saw them together,' I said, though I didn't know why I was telling him. Who was Dan Munro, except an unknowing catalyst who'd freed the past I hadn't wanted? Nothing but a stranger with an appealing voice and conservative good looks. He could have been anyone, I realised – anyone with a camera. What difference would it make if he knew? I told him anyway. 'Dracula asked Calanthe to go with him.'

Fake cobwebs shimmied above Dan's head like ghost

breath. He stayed where he was, his hands by his sides. He didn't reach for me again. 'Who's Calanthe?'

I huffed in annoyance that he wanted to know this detail. That that was his main concern. Everything always boiled down to Calanthe. She'd take over the story as though no one else was involved if I wasn't careful. 'He asked her to go with him,' I said, as though he hadn't heard me the first time. 'She said she'd think about it.'

'And?'

'Don't you get it?' Of course he didn't. I dragged my hands over my face, vividly recalling Dracula's suave demeanour. Comprehending only now just how dangerously Calanthe had lived. A foolish girl craving the flattery of predatory men. 'I need to find out who he was. What his name was. Where he lives.'

'Why's it so important?'

'Because I didn't tell anyone about what happened.' With this confession, a pain flared in my chest; a sharpness that dulled to a pulsating ache. 'I kept it to myself because I wanted her gone.' There, I'd said it. The absolute truth. After what I'd seen through the hole in the plaster hidden behind burning wallflowers, I'd wanted more than anything for Calanthe to go away. I thought if she did, my embarrassment would too. Even now, I could imagine her mocking voice taunting me: Frumpy Wilhelmina likes to watch.

Calanthe leaving had seemed like the perfect solution. But now, as a rational adult, it didn't seem right. Not as simple as I'd supposed all those years ago. I'd suppressed information so I could have a better life at The Zoltan. Just me and Aunt Lyrica. But at what cost?

I felt dizzyingly sick as all of this truth laid itself bare.

What have I done?

'I have to get back to The Zoltan,' I said, pushing past Dan and stumbling through the remaining maze of corridors till a glowing green EXIT sign marked the way out. I exploded outside to the rear of the building, the cold, sharp air stinging my airways. Then I ran, pitching my way along Pier Road, up Khyber Pass, then taking the steps to the whale bones two at a time. My lungs burned and my throat felt scorched with every laboured, ragged breath I took, but I didn't let up. I needed to know Dracula's true identity.

Unnerving silence shrouded The Zoltan when I arrived. Dread coated every surface and bit of incense-infused air with a palpable weightiness. Warmth from the radiator caught at the back of my throat, making me double over in a coughing fit. My panting breaths were hoarse and painful, but I stumbled onwards along the hallway. When I passed the dining room, which lay in relative darkness, I didn't dare look inside to see what was on the canvas on the chimneybreast wall. My mind would no doubt cause a distraction. Mutilated body parts or the leering form of Tom Dockin. *Snip snip snip.* A distraction from the task in hand. A distraction from the truth, which was perhaps much worse than the hallucinations themselves.

I continued through to the kitchen. Kevin cracked his eyes open, but didn't get up from his basket to greet me. Shameful behaviour, Catherine, I imagined him saying. What would your Aunt Lyrica and Uncle Ged think?

'I know, I know, I know,' I said, agitated, swiping the key to the cellar door from the hook above the breakfast bar and rushing back out to the hallway, to the door behind the staircase.

The vampire paced the floor of Room One. Emaciated. Barely able to breathe. Hurry, hurry, hurry, it wheezed.

My fingers were like strips of marshmallow as I tried to insert the key in the lock.

What am I supposed to do if I find his name? I thought, hoping I'd find it, but also hoping I wouldn't.

Take it to the police, the vampire said.

But it's information I've withheld for *sixteen years.*

Better late than never.

Will I be in trouble?

The vampire sat on the edge of the bed. Worry about that later.

The lock turned. I pulled open the door. A cloying smell of old building wafted upwards, smothering my face like a compress of damp, soiled rags. I reached inside, my fingers finding the light switch on the gritty, uncovered brickwork. When I pressed it, a faint glow highlighted the bottom of the stairs. A shock of bugs scattered across boards and bricks, disappearing into black gaps and crevices till none remained.

I gripped the banister. My feet suddenly didn't want to move. What I was about to do might change everything irreversibly.

Are you sure about this?

The vampire sighed. What are you waiting for?

I'm scared.

Too late for that.

But…

Just do it!

Each wooden stair creaked as I descended. At the bottom, the cellar lay like a dingy rectangle of neat abandonment. A storage place for all the things Aunt Lyrica wanted to keep, but out of sight. Silver filing cabinets and stacked cardboard boxes lined most of the wall space, and Uncle Ged's drum kit dwelt in a dusty, shadowy pocket of stasis in the corner.

'Your conscience finally got the better of you?' Calanthe said. She was leaning against the closest filing cabinet, regarding me with one eye. The other was missing. Where it used to be, a vacuous hole allowed insects to access her skull.

I wasn't even startled to see her. 'Evening, Calanthe.'

'Is your guilt a heavy, troublesome thing?' Her throat made a wet gurgling sound as she spoke. A significant portion of her neck gaped open. The stumps of her arms bled onto the floor. 'Is it becoming too much to bear?'

'Shut up,' I said, stepping closer to the filing cabinets, determined not to be cowed. 'It was your own doing.'

Calanthe stood up straight, her smirk widening. 'Go on then,' she said, nodding to the second filing cabinet along from the right. 'Find the guestbook you came to see. 2003. Twelfth of April.'

'I know when it was.' How could I ever forget? It was the day Summer was born. The day Dracula stayed in Room Three. And the day Calanthe disappeared.

'Flip through its pages and see in black and white the name of my killer.'

'So he did murder you?'

Calanthe groaned. 'I was always blindsided by your drabness. I mean, you're so uninspiring to look at. Even in velvet, you're about as appealing as beige on beige. But I underestimated you. We were more alike than I ever thought possible.'

'We were never alike.' I opened the filing cabinet and trailed my finger along the spines of old guest books.

'When you learn the truth, you'll realise you're wrong.'

'What truth?'

'You'll see.' Calanthe sidled closer. 'You already see the insects he sends you, but you don't eat them. Not yet. I think you will when you figure this whole thing out, though. You'll take all he offers.'

'Do you know how crazy you sound?'

'Yet it's you I can picture in Renfield's strait jacket. It's the right colour for your washed-out complexion.'

'You aren't even here,' I told her. I found the guest book for 2003 and slid it out. It felt dangerous in my hands.

Calanthe breathed on my neck. 'Oh, I'll always be here, my dearest Wilhelmina.'

'Then perhaps I'm losing my mind.'

Ha ha ha, said the vampire.

'You make it sound like there's still hope for you.' Calanthe laughed. 'Yet you're already twice as mad as you ever hoped not to be.'

I flicked through the pages of the book. The pressure of many black biro inscriptions embossed each one. I ran my fingers over some of them. Names, addresses and dates felt like braille against my fingertips.

April. April. April.

Twelfth of April.

Room Three.

There we go.

That's…

No no no.

'Everything you need to know, right there,' Calanthe said in my ear. 'Another jumpstart for your bottled-up memories, the ones that needed more coaxing.'

My eyes glittered. I blinked rapidly. Felt the book slipping from my hands, felt my legs giving way.

'Surely you remember everything now? Surely that's all the help you need to piece it together?' Calanthe urged. 'Like I said, it was the most impressive thing you ever did.'

20

Catherine Hall

2019

I could feel heavy man-breath on my face, hear the intermittent grate of metal, the raggedness of diseased airways. The legend of Tom Dockin was real. He was closer than ever before. As near as the promise of death wrapped in delirium, making my skin sweat and chill. My black wings trembled beneath me, broken. Velveteen feathers no use to me now. Tom Dockin's strong jawbone worked rhythmically, as if reinforcing the effort made by his ancient but durable lungs to breathe. Poisoned carbon dioxide poured from his scabby lips straight up my nostrils and into my lungs. Clean oxygen which I might have breathed was sucked inside him only to be spoiled. Every inhalation and exhalation he made came through his mouth, exposing the raw stink of putrefied gums along the ridges of which were pointed iron veneers, styled by whatever masochist dentist had thought to screw them into his monstrous skull. These veneers threatened my exposed skin and hidden nerve endings with untold pain.

He'll make you scream, my mother had told me more than once in the past. But had this folkloric hearsay scared or thrilled her? I was no longer sure.

Well, Mother, I'm screaming now. Albeit silently. Is that good enough?

Will it satisfy his sadistic intent?

WILL IT?

The total reek of the bogeyman filled my nose and mouth, attaching itself to my skin and hair, burrowing into my pores, binding itself with all of me.

'Have you come for my soul?' I asked.

'Cat?' Fingers dug into my upper arms, shaking me with abrupt force. I opened my eyes and saw Dan Munro. 'Did you fall?' he asked, his face a surprise. I'd expected to see the Devil's eyes staring back. 'Are you okay?'

'Mmn.' I wasn't sure. Would I ever be?

He reached across and picked the guestbook off the floor, some of its pages now creased.

I sat up. The room span with its swirls of blood all over the walls, as though Calanthe had crawled all over them. My hands were red. 'Look at the twelfth of April,' I said, my heart crashing, pumping more infected blood everywhere. Inside my skin, but also not.

Dan scanned the pages. When he found the right one, he trawled down the list of entries. 'What am I looking for?'

'Room Three. Read the name of the person who stayed there.'

'Mike Brandling.'

What? I couldn't comprehend the noise Dan had made with his mouth and tongue. It wasn't what I'd expected. His enunciation had had the right amount of syllables, but it sounded wrong. Less harsh than it should. 'No.' I shook my head. 'That's not right.'

'It's definitely Mike Brandling. Here, look.' Dan swivelled the guestbook, his forefinger marking the capitalised entry to save me the bother of finding it.

'But…'

'Who did you think stayed there?' He closed the book as though my thoughts didn't matter and its page's sneaky untruths were gospel. And maybe they were. But maybe they weren't.

I felt the darkness of The Zoltan pulsating all around

and inside me, an excited mass of demons waiting for me to verbalise their master's name as I'd seen it in black ink only moments before. Or had it been hours ago? Say it, say it, say it, they said.

'Tom Dockin.'

'Who's he?'

'The bogeyman.'

Dan grunted. Raised an eyebrow in irritation, as though I'd asked him to do me a favour he couldn't refuse despite having better things to do. 'Dracula, you mean? You think he was the bogeyman and that he stayed in Room Three?'

'Yes, but no. And yes.' I punctuated each word with my hands. 'I was completely wrong. You see, all this time I've hidden a mistaken secret. The real one is much worse. And I hid that too.' I laughed at the preposterous lead up to my great revelation. Sitting on the dusty cellar floor of The Zoltan, a part of the building barely trodden. How appropriate it was, yet utterly disappointing. The truth was more insane than I could have imagined. Wilder than anything Calanthe could have dreamt up.

My dearest Wilhelmina, it was the most impressive thing you ever did.

'Mike Brandling looked like Dracula,' I said, 'but he wasn't the bogeyman. He might have been a lesser version, I'll give him that, but he wasn't the *real* one. He was just a man. A self-doubting man who liked to lure the likes of Calanthe with his gimmicks and supposed worldliness. All he wanted was for the world to fall in love with him, to be awed by his greatness, so in return he could fuck it. He was beautiful after all, but in the end he was nothing but a scapegoat.'

Dan narrowed his eyes. Failed to realise the enormity of what had happened here at The Zoltan sixteen years ago. 'Whose scapegoat?'

I tried to climb to my feet but couldn't quite manage it, my legs too shaky. 'Mine.'

Dan took my hands and heaved me upwards. His hands were cool and strong, the kind that would be good in a crisis. Well good, I thought, this is quite the disaster. Some blood from my hands transferred to his, but he didn't seem to notice. The room span faster. We were in a large empty hall, no fixtures or fittings, dancing at a masquerade ball which we'd invited no one else to. Hundreds of cats' eyes blinked like cameras flashing.

You'd look good on my walls.

Likewise, darling.

'I don't know what you're talking about,' Dan said, pulling his hands from mine and gripping my arms and slowing the room till it came to a grinding halt. I almost fell into him. Would he care if I did? I wondered. Would he mind if I slipped into his skin? A sense of badness coursed through me, as if to take ownership.

I'd like to climb to the top of your summit and taste the air from its highest peak.

'Cat?' Dan shook me to remind me he was there. Not that I needed reminding. His eyes held me captive.

'Calanthe was right,' I said, breathing hard, unable to subdue the involuntary grin that crept to my mouth. 'It was the most impressive thing I ever did. It wasn't Mike Brandling, see. And it doesn't matter what's written there in the book, not really, because Calanthe showed me the name I needed to see and now I remember what happened.'

'Cat, seriously…'

'It was all my fault. I did it. Me.'

'Did what?' Dan's grip slackened. His strikingly normal face seemed to melt with uncertainty. Perhaps some of me had fallen into him, my heated excitement burning him from the inside out.

I'm dangerous, I warned, the words not leaving my head. 'I made her disappear.'

Dan scratched his chin and shuffled backwards. 'Would

you, er, like me to try calling your aunt or something?' he suggested.

'No!'

'Well, I dunno… how about a doctor?'

'I don't need a doctor either.' *Doctor, you don't know what it is to doubt everything, even yourself.* 'There's nothing anyone can do. It's too late.'

Dan seemed to mistake this as an observation of the time. 'Then maybe I can help you to your room? You don't seem well. You should probably lie down. Get some rest. I can stay here till your aunt gets back, if you like? So you're not alone.'

Loneliness will sit over our roofs with brooding wings.

Not broken ones though. Oh no. Richly glossy two-tone wings that change colour with the light, snaring all kinds of attention from those who'd rather not see. Flitting promiscuously and hypnotically now and then because it's such a slut.

Are you lonely, Dan Munro?

'Yes, that would be good.' I allowed him to guide me up the cellar's narrow staircase to the hallway, my feet practically floating. I imagined we were in Transylvania, trapped in the maze of Dracula's Castle. Endless flights of stairs. Unknown danger round every corner. The hall light could easily be a flickering candle in a wrought iron wall sconce, I thought, only it wasn't flickering. And Kevin might be Zoltan in the guise of a small terrier. He might well kill us. He might just as easily not.

'When I first saw you,' I said to Dan, as he steered me along the hallway to the stairs to the first floor, 'I would have sworn we'd already met. In the past. Somewhere else.'

There was movement at the top of the stairs. Floorboards creaking, someone crawling into view. Calanthe. She perched herself on the top stair, watching our ascent. All four of her limbs were missing now. She was a perfect, bloodied torso balancing precariously on the edge of final ruin. Dan didn't seem to notice. He shook his head and said, 'I'm pretty sure we've never met before.'

'In a different lifetime, I think we knew each other extremely well.' I nodded my growing certainty on the matter.

'You reckon?'

'Definitely. We built sandcastles together.'

'Um, okay.'

Calanthe roared with laughter and almost fell backwards. 'Sandcastles? You're such a fucking riot, Wilhelmina.'

I glared at her, willing her to die all over again. 'Shut your stupid face.'

'Excuse me?' Dan turned his face to me, shocked.

'Oh, sorry, I didn't mean you.' I pointed at Calanthe. 'Can't you see her there?'

Dan looked to the top of the stairs, then back at me and shook his head. 'See who?'

I smiled, happy with his answer. 'No one. It really doesn't matter.'

Calanthe hissed and folded to the floor and slithered away from us. She propped herself against the door to Room Three, slack-jawed, like a crime scene re-enactment. Her remaining eye rolled back in its socket and her missing limb stumps bled on the carpet. The same blood was on my hands. I'd transferred it from mine to Dan's and it had crept up the sleeves of his coat. Ugly reddish black stains.

'Right, well, here we are,' he said when we reached the door to my room.

I was scared that he'd leave me, and that would be that, so I told him, 'I asked Tom Dockin to take her away.'

If Dan was shocked, he didn't show it. 'Calanthe? The girl you keep mentioning?'

'Yes. She was my cousin. I was angry with her and it was the only thing I could think to do.'

'You're saying you asked the bogeyman to take your cousin away and you actually think he did?'

'In a way, yes.'

'In a way?'

'What I mean is that he ate her up. He has metal teeth, see. That's what he does. He eats people. Bad people.'

Dan reached out and opened the door to my room, exhaling loudly as he did.

'It's true,' I said. 'He ate her up because she was bad. Also because I asked him to.' This particular detail delighted me. 'And he's here again. I've seen him.'

Without a word, Dan gestured for me to go inside. His feet stayed planted firmly where he stood, as though he feared the unlit room. That perhaps it would suck him in and never let him out.

'If I wanted, I could ask him to take my little sister too,' I said, unmoving.

'Shouldn't you look out for your little sister?' I felt Dan's hand in the middle of my back, applying firm but gentle pressure. He pushed me into the gloom where the vampire's presence was a silent scream with no teeth. Then he switched on the light. Cockroaches scurried up the walls, and I saw why the vampire was so quiet. Dead and decomposing, it was lying in a festering mess of its own fluids on top of the bed. Its putrid stink filled me up. I unbuttoned Calanthe's cloak and cast it over its remains so Dan might not see.

'I wouldn't really ask him to take Summer,' I said.

'I should think not.' Dan's brow creased as he surveyed the messiness of my room. 'She's just a wee girl.'

I sat on the edge of the bed and rung my hands together and knew this time he would leave and I'd probably never see him again. 'Would you kiss me good night before you go, Dan Munro?' I giggled at the unintended rhyme, enjoying the feel of his name on my tongue.

He shook his head. His mouth a straight line.

'Why not?'

'I'm married.'

'You're not wearing a ring.'

'But I have a wife.'

'Are you separated?'

His eyes flared with annoyance.

'Supposing you didn't have a wife,' I said, kicking off my boots and lying back, so my head rested on the pillow, 'would you kiss me then?'

'No.'

'Why not?'

'Just go to sleep.'

'Why not? Because I'm ugly?'

'I don't know you.'

'You didn't know your wife at some point either.'

'Just go to sleep, Cat,' he said, retreating to the landing. 'I'll be downstairs.' The door clicked shut, and I heard his feet on the stairs. I glanced around the room. He'd left some of his bad mood to fester like shadows. It grew. It breathed.

21

Lyrica Black

2019

It was just after nine when Lyrica and Summer arrived back at The Zoltan. Good spirits, the sort that transfer from other people in lively social environments, had remedied the worst of nostalgia. There'd been a contagious sense of togetherness at the restaurant because it was almost Christmas. Drinking wine and being around others, albeit a room full of strangers, had made Lyrica braver. She dared to think Sister Gregory's visitations had been some Dickensian style psychology. The festive season is a time for reflection, after all, especially in the wake of a sibling's untimely passing.

'How about Home Alone?' Summer said, marching into the B&B and taking some of the freshness of outside with her.

'If you can find it, we'll watch it.' Lyrica closed the front door and shrugged out of her coat. 'I'll put the kettle on while you have a look in the TV cabinet.' As she followed Summer along the hallway, a shadowy figure emerged from the dining room, making her jump. 'Jesus Christ.'

'Sorry.' It was Dan Munro. Room Two. Her only paying guest. 'Can I have a word?'

'Yeah, of course.' Lyrica could tell straight away that something bad had happened, something that would kill outright the temporary cheer she'd found at Portofino's. His countenance was too serious and there was a distraught pallor about his face which she hadn't noticed before. The corded phone to her right rang out, an aggressive shrillness that made her jolt again, interrupting their exchange and jangling her nerves more. 'Sorry, do you mind if I...?' She pointed to the phone.

Dan shook his head. He looked disappointed, but gestured with both hands for her to *go ahead*.

Lyrica maintained his gaze as she picked up the receiver, spiny intuition telling her this wouldn't be welcome news either. 'The Zoltan, how may I help?'

'Lyrica?'

'Oh. Patrick?' She realised she shouldn't be surprised that he was calling, but was all the same.

'Did Catherine tell you I'd called?'

'No. When was this?'

'This morning.'

'Must have slipped her mind. What's up? Is it about Summer?' Lyrica rolled her eyes. What now? She watched Dan turn and retreat into the gloom of the dining room, a polite but false perception of giving her some privacy.

'So Catherine *did* tell you?'

'Tell me what?' Lyrica clamped a hand to her forehead. Conversations with Patrick were never easy. 'She's hardly said anything today. She's not feeling well.'

'I called around eleven-ish to ask if Summer was there. Catherine said she wasn't, so I asked her to let me know if she showed up. I'm beside myself with worry here, Lyrica, and I thought you of all people might have called back to check if there'd been any developments.'

The underside of Lyrica's face zinged with an unpleasant coldness, making it feel not real, as though her skin was a latex mask and would peel from the outside edges, revealing the petrified remains of Maureen Hall beneath. 'But Summer is here. She said that you…'

'Summer's there? With you? Now?'

'Yes. She arrived this morning. We must have been out shopping when you called. I took her for a meal this evening. We've only just got back. I thought you knew where she was.'

'No, I bloody didn't.' His voice was a booming crescendo of outrage.

'Ah.'

'I tried calling her this morning, to remind her to come straight home after college, but she'd turned her mobile off. So I called the college, to get someone to pass on the message. They called me back shortly afterwards to tell me she'd not shown up. I went home and found some of her stuff was missing. I've been calling all over the place since. Friends. Neighbours. I've had the police out too. And all this time she's been… with *you?*'

Lyrica felt the ground tilt beneath her feet. Saw the flash of a newspaper headline in her head: Girl of Sixteen Runs Away from Home. Not again. The lamp on the table flickered and dimmed. Her guts twisted painfully – carbonara, tiramisu and wine threatening to make a comeback.

Mary had a little lamb. Mary had a little lamb.

'Keep her there where you can damn well see her,' Patrick said. 'I'm coming to get her.'

'Now?'

'Yes, now.'

'Why don't you let her stay the night? I'll talk to her. You can come for her first thing in the morning.'

Patrick's rage was practically audible, filling the phone line with a ferociousness she wasn't used to. Not from a man, in any case. Never a man. Lyrica cringed.

'She can't just run off and do whatever she likes,' he said. 'She has to learn this is *not* acceptable.'

'But still…'

'She's *my* daughter, Lyrica. She belongs at home with *me*.'

She's not a possession, Lyrica wanted to tell him. But she didn't, because the accusation in his voice was clear, perhaps even true: You weren't even capable of looking after your own daughter.

'I'll be there within the hour.' Patrick hung up.

Lyrica replaced the receiver in its cradle and leant against the wall, closing her eyes. Sister Gregory's words sprang to mind: You'd better pray he doesn't come for her.

Perhaps it was for the best that Patrick came and took Summer away. Compared with Tom Dockin he was by far the lesser of two evils. All around and above and beneath her, dark shadows breathed and swelled and quietly recited stories that were best left forgotten. Shadows Lyrica hoped her younger niece hadn't been exposed to already. Let it stop here, she thought. Let Summer be free from the nightmares of Eden House.

When she opened her eyes again, Dan Munro was standing in the doorway to the dining room, shrouded in shadow, watching her. He'd put on his coat and hat. Seemed keen to leave.

'Sorry about that.' Lyrica pushed herself off the wall, forcing a smile. 'What was it you wanted to…?'

'It's about Cat,' he said, stepping into the hall. Into the light. 'I don't really know how to say this, but… something's not right with her.'

Lyrica felt the floor shift beneath her again. 'How do you mean? Did something happen?'

'When I came back earlier, I found her lying on the floor in the cellar. I helped her up to her room, but she was talking gibberish.'

'In what way?'

'I dunno, she was spouting some weird stuff about Room Three and someone called Tom Dockin. Calanthe too.'

'Calanthe? What about her?'

Dan shrugged and made eyes as if to say *None of my business, sorry. Wish I hadn't got involved.*

'Is she okay? Cat, I mean.'

'Listen, I don't know. Go up and see her for yourself. Like I say, she wasn't making much sense. I mean, she thought I was Dracula.' He headed to the front door and pulled it open. An icy blast of wind swiped down the hall and wrapped itself around Lyrica. 'Oh, and I'll be heading off first thing in the morning,' he said, looking almost surprised by the admission, as though he'd only just decided and needed to make it known before his decisiveness got lost to whatever nonsensical transgressions he thought were culminating in The Zoltan. 'Don't worry about making me breakfast, I'll grab something on the road. Seems you have enough on your plate.' Then he was gone.

And everywhere that Mary went, Lyrica thought, Tom Dockin was sure to go.

'That was my dad on the phone, wasn't it?' Summer was standing at the other end of the hall, her arms folded over her chest. Not in a display of sulky indignation, but more in the way of someone who meant to guard themselves. She looked small. Childlike. Fearful.

Lyrica nodded. She tried to make a stern face, but it was little more than a wearied frown. 'You'd better gather your things together. He's coming for you soon.'

Summer didn't argue. 'Sorry for not telling you the truth,' she said. 'I figured you'd send me home if I did, and I don't want to go back.'

Lyrica's heart heaved. 'We'll talk about it later. I promise.' For now, as unlikely as it seemed, she had a more pressing issue to deal with. She inhaled deeply, braced herself, and looked to the stairs. Already she could hear snakes thrashing in the walls and beetles ticking on

unseen surfaces.
Cat, what have you done?

22

Catherine Hall

2019

Calanthe slithered around the room, leaving trails of blood on the carpet and walls like wet scorch marks. Reanimated, she plagued me, the remains of her mangled body unable to rest. Wouldn't stay dead.

'Couldn't even haggle a kiss,' she said, swiping her blueish black forked tongue across her bottom lip. Had it always been forked? I couldn't remember. Her words were spiked more often than not, so I thought it likely. 'Bet you couldn't buy one either, not even for a million pounds. Poor Wilhelmina, if you could only see yourself.'

I looked up, beyond the white plaster ceiling to the night sky. Polaris winked at me. Going north, lassie? Stick with me.

Do you have a wife?

Can't say that I do.

'Cat?' There was a soft rapping like cat paws on my face, then the door opened and Aunt Lyrica walked in bringing with her a burst of celestial light. 'Are you all right?'

All right? What does that even mean?

I tried to sit up, but the bed half ate me. I wriggled in its metal coils.

I thought I might have you all to myself, I imagined myself saying, the words not developed enough for her to understand. Calanthe didn't deserve you. She got what she deserved.

Aunt Lyrica sat on the edge of the bed, her skin glowing white, hurting my eyes with its radiance. 'What's going on? Dan just spoke to me, he said you aren't well. That he found you in the cellar. What were you doing down there?'

I covered my eyes with my fingers. Her beauty was too blinding. 'He's not Dracula, you know.'

'I didn't think for a second he was.' Aunt Lyrica touched my arm. Her hand melted into my skin. 'What's this all about?'

'He reminded me of a man I once met,' I said, marvelling at the way my arm joined her wrist. 'Someone who dressed as Dracula. He had a camera like Dan and was staying at The Zoltan the day Calanthe disappeared.'

Aunt Lyrica pulled away. Our skin stretched like hot mozzarella, then snapped, and we became two separate entities again. Without moving her mouth, she asked, why are you doing this?

'His name was Mike Brandling. He stayed in Room Three.' I climbed out of the mattress and sat up, too exhausted to control my tongue. 'I checked the guest book. His name was there. Not at first, but it's there now.'

'What are you going on about? And what does it matter what his name was?'

'Because…' Tell her. Don't do it. *Tell her!* 'I thought he might have taken Calanthe.'

'Why would you think that?' Aunt Lyrica's face became a smudged white disc.

'Because she slept with him after he asked her to go with him.'

'Don't be ridiculous.'

'It's true. I saw them. I heard.' Just shut up shut up shut up.

'But… why are you telling me this only now?'

'Because… I don't know.' It was my knowledge to keep. My dirty secret. Except I realise now it wasn't. 'It doesn't really matter anymore. I know he didn't take her.' Just leave it alone, I begged. You're picking at the scabs and they aren't ready to come off yet and my words will come out like blood and stain everything.

'Mike Brandling? I agree, it's not possible that he could have taken her. The police followed up with everyone who'd stayed here that weekend.' Aunt Lyrica shook her head as if what I'd told her hadn't sunk in. 'There were no leads.'

I'd never known that before. Why didn't I know that?

'But I don't understand,' Aunt Lyrica persisted. 'Why are you saying these things now? If you had other information, if you knew there was a chance…'

'There is no chance. He didn't take her.'

'But… How do you know?' Aunt Lyrica's voice became sharp with building hysteria. It threatened to shatter my brain like a china pot, grey-veined with fragility. And if it was to shatter, I realised no one would ever know what I knew. My secret would stay a secret.

I waited for her to say more. For my brain to explode. But she didn't, and it didn't, so I said, 'Tom Dockin took her.'

'Don't you dare do this.'

'Mum talked about Tom Dockin,' Summer announced. She'd crept up the stairs and was standing at the open door, backpack slung over her shoulder (she was leaving!) and a small book held tightly in her arms, pressed to her chest (guarding secrets of her own?). She was a heavenly image, one to be eternalised on stained glass for people to look at and be awed by.

Everyone loves Summer.

'Doesn't it seem too much of a coincidence that you were born on the day Calanthe died?' I said.

When Summer didn't respond, I wondered if I'd spoken

at all. Insects marched a timeless beat inside the walls. Inside my head.

'Perhaps you're the reincarnation of her,' I suggested.

'Stop that.' Aunt Lyrica looked from me to Summer, then back again. Her blue eyes had turned black. Inkwells in her skull. 'I can't believe this,' she said, her mouth moving wetly and angrily. 'It's been sixteen years since Calanthe disappeared and in all that time you've known things that no one else did, but you said nothing. *Why?*' Ink ran down her cheeks. Veins in marble.

Why was I never enough? That's what I wanted to ask in my own hysterical way. But I didn't. We were seeking answers to our own questions and we shouldn't lest we discovered something worse than the pain we'd learned to live with.

'You were right about her being here,' I said, hoping to fix what I'd broken. We could all exist in the same space if that's what Aunt Lyrica truly wanted. If that's what it would take for me to stay: Calanthe a mutilated torso, still more beautiful than I, and me a fungus breathing and living in the shade. 'I've seen her.'

'Don't lie to me,' Aunt Lyrica warned.

'It's true.'

'Did she speak to you?' Summer asked, moving closer, morbid curiosity casting diamonds in her eyes. 'Did she tell you what happened?'

'Yes, Tom Dockin ate her up.'

Aunt Lyrica was a blur. Her hand slapped my face before I saw it. My brain still didn't shatter.

'You were always blinkered to the things she did,' I said, touching my cheek, not feeling my fingers upon it. 'She was always lying to you. Stealing and drinking. Taking drugs, too. And do you realise how many men she had on the go?' I laughed spitefully. 'Notice I said men, not boys.' I realised I was saying things that couldn't be retracted, but these hurts were too deep and sore, too aggravated by far to stay inside, each detail spewing out like a stinking infection no one wanted to clean or dress. The truth was being extracted. Amputated. 'You were downstairs watching *Murder, She Wrote* that day while she was in Room Three. She was draped across the bed while Dracula took pictures of her naked body.'

'You're lying.' Aunt Lyrica said this with no conviction.

'It's true. And I think part of her only screwed him to spite me.'

'Don't be so crude.' Aunt Lyrica jumped to her feet, as though my nearness suddenly repelled her. 'I'm going to call the police now, and you're going to tell them what you remember about that day.'

'But it's pointless.' I felt the bed dragging me down again, into its metal belly. 'I already told you what happened.'

Aunt Lyrica's eyes flared blacker. 'You'll tell them the truth, do you hear me?'

'That Tom Dockin ate her because I asked him to?'

'Enough!'

'He's here at The Zoltan too, you know.' I gripped the headboard for leverage. To stop myself from being eaten alive. 'I've seen him. My mother brought him the day of Uncle Ged's funeral. Remember? Did he ever really leave?'

'Your mother was sick.'

'Aren't we all? It's a family curse.'

Aunt Lyrica made a scornful noise in her throat. 'I'm beginning to think you're the sickest of us all.'

'You didn't know Calanthe all that well, did you?'

Aunt Lyrica inhaled this new hurt with a sharp intake. 'After you've spoken to the police,' she said, 'I want you to go. You're not welcome here anymore.' The inkwells in her face dilated and contracted like blowholes. 'What you've done is unforgivable. Your mother was right, you're an abomination.' She blustered from the room in a blurry cloud of white and black and red.

Abomination. My mind explored this word, my tongue silently tripping over each syllable. It looked and sounded meek despite having such a significant, scathing definition. I felt nothing but indifferent to it.

Summer unfolded her arms and threw the small book at me. 'Mum should have aborted you.'

23

Jeanette Hall's Diary

28th January 1986

Maureen's been gone only a month. It feels much longer. She comes back to visit each week, and when she does she's like a trapped butterfly, all skittish and restless, and I know she can't wait to get out again.

Less than ten months till you're free, she reminded me this morning. Feels like a life time. We considered for a while I might get out sooner if she acted as my guardian, but she has no means to support us both yet. She temps (mostly bar work, which I'm too young to do) and rents a room in someone's house. For now, you're better off staying here, she said. It's not easy out there, and I need to find my feet. By the time you join me we'll be flying though. Just keep your nose clean and don't do anything to piss Sister Gregory off.

That doesn't take much, I reminded her.

My knuckles are still sore off Mr Birchwood's kiss two weeks ago, when I dropped a pile of freshly laundered sheets on the floor.

Hey, at least you'll be out for Christmas, Maureen said, as if that should spur me on and give me strength.

I hate Christmas.

4th February 1986

Maureen visited today. She's dyed her hair red (!) and her skin is, for want of a better word, glowing. She looks so healthy. She says she wants to change her name by deed poll. Has this big idea of recreating herself and erasing the Eden House days. I told her to do whatever she feels is right and made out I was happy about her plan. I don't think it's as simple as that though. No amount of name changing, hair-colouring or moving can change what happened here. It'll always stay with us. Besides, Mum and Dad gave her that name, it's all she has left of them. I'll always be Jeanette.

Anyway, no wonder Maureen seems perkier this week. She's met a man! He's called Ged Black. They got chatting while she was working at a bar in the city centre, and they've been on a date already. He took her to the seaside (!) on the back of his motorbike (!) and bought her fish & chips (!) I can't even imagine! She showed me a photo of him and, although he looks quite a bit older than her, he's handsome. He owns a B&B in Whitby. Whitby! Maureen said he reckons there's plenty of work there and that she should visit him sometime soon. I think she will.

In Eden House news, there was a bit of drama last night. Sister Gregory marched Joanna Blakelock out of the dorm, all because she got blood on her sheets and was crying hysterically. I don't know where Joanna was taken or what happened to her, but she hasn't spoken a word since. All I know is that Sister Gregory told Joanna that Tom Dockin's like a shark and would most certainly come for her.

Maybe he did.

Father Morris's replacement arrived yesterday. He looks quite young and, although I've not talked to him, seems pleasant. Father Morris was really old and too wrapped up in religion and tradition to care about the humanity of this place. I wonder, therefore, if this new vicar will be a good thing. Maybe I can speak to him about some things that go on here.

We'll see.

I can't stop thinking about poor Joanna Blakelock.

6th *February 1986*

I asked Father Corrigan (that's the name of the new vicar) if he'd like me to stack the hymn books and glue any of their loose pages after service this morning, just so I could try to get a feel for what he's like. He accepted my offer appreciatively, then hung around chatting for a while. He's really nice. We talked about trivial things, mostly. I asked if we might get some modern women's literature for the library, because at the moment it's all old stuff by men, probably old men at that. He laughed at this, but said he'd see what he could do. If he speaks to Sister Gregory about it, he'll get nowhere. But I didn't feel I could say as much, not yet. I'm still testing the waters. I only hope if he speaks to her about it, he doesn't mention my name. I can already imagine the thrashing I'd get off Mr Birchwood for my 'impertinence'. I reckon modern women's fiction to Sister Gregory is akin to harpies' songs in ink.

We also talked about the peacock that turned up in the gardens of Eden House last week. No one knows where it came from or who it belongs to, but it looks as though it'll stick around – much to the annoyance of Sister Gregory. Too much of a wretched distraction, she said. I'm surprised she hasn't snared it and beaten it to death with her cane by now. Father Corrigan disagrees with her, thankfully. He said it's a blessed thing of beauty and that all God's creatures are welcome here. Or something like that anyway. Father Corrigan is very softly spoken. You have to concentrate to hear what he says. Sometimes I miss words. He seems confident and amiable enough, though. Quite friendly, in fact. He told me he envisioned good things for me as I finished the last of the hymn books, then patted me reassuringly on the shoulder. Maybe next time I'll be daring enough to discuss Sister

Gregory's unorthodox ways. Joanna Blakelock still hasn't spoken since the bloody sheet incident.

Might Father Corrigan be Eden House's saviour?

Watch this space.

9*th* *February 1986*

Saw Father Corrigan in service today. He looked at me and smiled. Finally, a friendly face! Albeit a plain one. I know it's very mean of me to say, but he's got very forgettable features. Wasn't exactly graced with good looks. His personality shines beyond his plainness though, and I think that is what will make him memorable. He is a kind soul, I think.

Sister Gregory came to the dorm this evening as I was making up my bed with clean linen and told me Father Corrigan would like to see me in the chapel. My heart raced like mad because I thought he might have mentioned the women's books to her and that I'd be in trouble. Surprisingly though, she delivered the message then left. (I feel as though I'll get some punishment later – she won't appreciate being a deliverer of messages).

I went to the chapel and found Father Corrigan in the side room, standing by a bookcase reading a book. Something about psychology, I think. Ah Jeanette, he said, I thought you might like to lend a hand re-covering the hymn books. I noticed how tired and battered they're looking, so I sourced some wallpaper cuttings from a shop in town to spruce them up a bit. They should do the job quite nicely, I think. Till we can fund some new ones, that is.

I told him I'd be happy to help.

He laughed and said, Yes, well, I imagine it'll be better than whatever chores Sister Gregory had in mind.

I almost blurted out, You don't know the half of it. But didn't.

We spent the next hour folding and taping bits of

wallpaper to the hymn books while chatting. The minutes flew and by the time we were tidying away I said it was just as well because it was getting late and I should get back. Father Corrigan agreed, then said, Won't be long till you can leave this fine establishment, I should imagine.

Less than ten months, I told him. Then I laughed and said, Not that I'm counting or anything.

Father Corrigan sighed and clasped his hands together. I suppose it's all down to the formalities of paperwork, isn't it? he said. Because, technically, you're already a woman.

I nodded in agreement, but felt embarrassed. Really, I feel no different or wiser or worldlier than when I was, say, fourteen or fifteen.

Perhaps you'd like to help me again tomorrow evening, he suggested, when I stood up to go.

But we've finished them all, I said, pointing at the stack of madly floral hymn books (which Sister Gregory will no doubt despise).

Believe me, he said laughing, there are lots of things that need to be taken care of round here.

Ha! If only Father Morris could hear him say that! I told him okay, then left, feeling in some way happier. It's as though Father Corrigan is throwing me a lifeline. Maybe soon I'll be brave enough to talk to him in confidence about more serious things.

12th May 1986

I've been quiet on the diary front lately, not because there's not much to report. Just I haven't had time. Maureen is living in Whitby with Ged Black now and they're planning to get married. She isn't wasting any time at all! A registry office wedding with minimal fuss, apparently. Ged's been married before, and neither of them is religious. So it's good enough for them, Maureen says. She also says she's changing her name to Lyrica. So that means when she's married, she'll be called Lyrica Black. Sounds like a film star's name. I'm so happy for her.

Joanna Blakelock still hasn't spoken yet. As you can imagine, rumours are rife. Michelle Curry says she saw her in the showers and that she had bruises like teeth marks all over her legs. Michelle Curry is known for making up stories though. All I know is that Joanna looks haunted. Whatever happened to her that night, it wasn't right.

There's some renovation work going on in the kitchen at the moment. Quite a few workmen come and go throughout the day. It's nice having people from the outside amongst us. The nuns are better behaved. In fact, I hope the overhaul takes ages to complete! There's this one workman in particular who doesn't look much older than me. An apprentice, most likely. He's really good looking, and as I was carrying a tray of dirty crockery into the kitchen, he winked at me. Maybe I'll find an excuse to collect the plates after lunch again tomorrow!

13*th* May 1986

Saw the apprentice again today, this time in the dining room. He was checking the electrics, I think. He said hello and when I said hello back he came over to talk to me. Right confident, like. His name is David Jones, and he has the most gorgeous green eyes. His hair's almost black and when he smiles he has this dimple that shows on his left cheek. He's nineteen and is training to be an electrician. I could have stood talking to him all day looking into his eyes had Sister Abbott not passed by and told me to stop standing around twittering. I suspect the news will get back to Sister Gregory. I dread to think what she'll do.

...

Sister Gregory came to the dorm this evening, but she said nothing to me. Phew! With any luck, Sister Abbott forgot to mention that she caught me chatting with one of the workmen and it will have slipped her mind by now.

15th May 1986

Saw David Jones again today. He asked if I'd like to go out with him some time on a date! I told him chance would be a fine thing. No way would Sister Gregory allow that. He looked disappointed. So I told him I won't be here for much longer, that I'll be free to do whatever I like by late November. He smiled, but I could tell he thought I was fobbing him off. As if! Maybe I could meet you in the yard some time, I said, surprising myself with how forward I sounded. David grinned and nodded and said, All right.

Oh. My. Word!

19th May 1986

Met David Jones in the yard today, round the back of the bin shelter. We talked for about fifteen minutes, and he shared a cigarette with me. He's SO nice and chatty and tall. He's lived in Sheffield his whole life and lives with his parents and three sisters. They have a dog – and a budgie too. He has straight teeth and smells nice. Clean and manly, like. We arranged to meet in the same place tomorrow.

I keep thinking I'll wake up and realise it was all just a wild dream. But I don't think it is, because before we left the bin shelter, David leaned in and kissed me, and as he did, I gripped the wooden rail which had a nail sticking out of it and it went straight into the fleshy part of my palm. It hurt. A lot. And bled. But I didn't wake up. And I didn't much care either, not when David was breathing life into me.

It's really silly, I know, but a childish part of me can't

help but think Jeanette Jones has a nice ring to it.

27ᵗʰ May 1986

I've been seeing David every day now, always behind the bins. Not exactly romantic, I know. But at least behind the bins we aren't under the watchful eye of Sister Gregory. She flicked Mr Birchwood across my ankles yesterday for dragging my heels across the floor, even though I wasn't. I'm sure she had her reasons. Whatever they were, I didn't notice the pain as much as I usually would have because I imagined being with David.

When I'm with him, we could be anywhere. He's so funny and kind and interesting. Not that I have anything to gauge it on, but he's a brilliant kisser too. And when he cuddles me, I want him to never let go. This has been the best week of my life by far.

In other news, Sister Gregory hit a girl in the face with Mr Birchwood after dinner this evening, breaking her nose. Prior to being smacked in the face, the girl had back-chatted. But that's beside the point. Sister Gregory can't be allowed to get away with this, so I finally plucked up the courage and went to speak to Father Corrigan, telling him about Sister Gregory's methods of punishment. At first he pooh-poohed the idea, saying she can't possibly be as bad as I was making out, but when I got upset and showed him some of the scars on my legs, he told me he believed me and that I was to leave it with him and he'd think on how best to tackle the situation.

At last! I should have done this weeks ago. Not to worry though, help is now at hand.

28ᵗʰ May 1986

I was wrong. I am cursed. I don't even know if I can write this.

How can I?

No, I must. What happened needs to be documented.

At seven-thirty, Sister Abbott came to tell me Father Corrigan wanted to see me in the side room of the chapel. I found him there – with Sister Gregory. I knew as soon as I saw her I was in trouble.

Father Corrigan tells me you've been wagging your tongue, she said.

I looked at Father Corrigan for help, but he simply sat there straight-faced.

You know what happens to unruly children, don't you? Sister Gregory said.

I'm not a child, I told her, feeling braver in the presence of Father Corrigan.

Indeed, he said, nodding in agreement.

In the eyes of the law, you're still a child, Sister Gregory insisted.

In the eyes of Tom Dockin too, I suppose? I said.

Father Corrigan looked from me to Sister Gregory, confused. Who's Tom Dockin?

The bogeyman, I told him.

The bogeyman? Gracious me! He laughed. What's this about? He looked to Sister Gregory for an explanation.

Children need discipline, Sister Gregory said, her knuckles tightening around Mr Birchwood. They have to understand there are consequences for their actions.

Father Corrigan nodded. I don't disagree.

His flippant response horrified me.

But how can it be right to punish someone for tripping on a loose piece of carpet? I said, naming just one example. Five lashes across the back of the legs is a bit extreme for such a trivial mishap. Surely you can see that?

How else will you learn to be mindful and focussed? Sister Gregory said, her mouth having tightened.

But it's wrong, I argued.

What's wrong, Miss Hall, is that you've been tittle tattling.

Father Corrigan was watching me. He looked the same,

but I didn't recognise him at all.

Sister Gregory marched to the door. I could feel her anger like a fourth presence in the room. I'll leave you to handle this, Father, she said. She tipped her head, minutely, at Father Corrigan, then left without another word, closing the door behind her.

Surely you don't agree with her? I said, astounded.

How could I have read him so wrong? I thought he was on my side. I thought he was better than the nuns.

We all could do with being a little more mindful and focussed, don't you think? Father Corrigan said, his voice especially low. And she's right that people must face up to the consequences of their actions. He got up from his seat and walked to the door and locked it.

What do you mean? I said. And what are you doing?

Father Corrigan came to stand in front of me. His eyes were unkind, in such a way I'd never seen them before, and they never left mine. People have reported seeing you in the yard with some boy, he said, his attention unyielding. I could tell he was angry. Is this true?

Yes, I said. There was no point lying.

And the pair of you have been fornicating behind the bins?

No, I said, feeling a wave of heated embarrassment rise to my face.

He regarded me for what felt like ages, his eyes stony cold. Do you want him to lose his job? he said at last.

Why would that happen? I asked.

For forcing himself on you.

But he never did.

Father Corrigan placed his hands on my shoulders. It's only a matter of time though, isn't it, Jeanette? The way you've been leading him on. He clicked his tongue and shook his head, suddenly breathing faster.

But... I haven't led him on, I said.

Haven't you? Father Corrigan laughed. It was an empty,

spiteful sound that made the hair on my neck prickle. I for one can vouch that you most certainly have, he said. And as Sister Gregory and I have both agreed, there must be consequences for your actions.

But I don't understand.

Come now, you and I both know you've led *me* on a merry little dance for weeks on end.

You?

And that's when he wrestled me to the desk and pinned me there with his terrible weight. His wet lips on my mouth. His nipping teeth at my neck. His clammy hands tearing at my clothes. I tried to cry out, but he clamped a hand over my mouth.

This is what you want, isn't it Jeanette? he said, grappling himself free from his trousers. Then he violated me in ways the nuns never had. Behind his hand I cried and screamed and prayed to the god who'd never listened that I'd die. I could smell Father Corrigan's meaty sweat, and feel the friction and pain of his thing jabbing me so forcefully, and the humility and defilement so intense, I thought I might pass out. He bucked and thrusted, faster and faster, and bit my shoulder so hard I thought he must have torn a chunk of my flesh free and taken it into his mouth. When he raised his head, I saw his face, and he was – Tom Dockin! His teeth were iron spears, coated with my blood, and his skin was heavily veined, almost translucent, as though he'd never seen daylight. His eyes were rolled back in their sockets. Blind, but seeing. The most terrible, fearsome, nightmarish part of my childhood – the bogeyman – was right there on top of me, grunting and panting and slavering through his unholy metal mouth. Groping with his hands. Crushing with his weight. Then after an indeterminable amount of time, he cried out and his body became rigid and he was suddenly Father Corrigan again. Red-faced, sweaty and ugly.

I can't decide if Father Corrigan or Tom Dockin raped

me. Maybe there's no difference. What happened is a mashed up nightmare in my head that I won't ever be able to forget. And I can't tell anyone about what happened either. Father Corrigan assured me: It's your word against mine. Besides, he said, Sister Gregory saw what that boy did to you behind the bin shelter. And you really wouldn't want him to lose his job and end up on some dubious register for the rest of his life, would you?

So I can't say anything. For David's sake. I just can't.

I can't see him again either. Not ever.

24th June 1986

I am carrying the Devil's child.

24

Catherine Hall

2019

So, I am the Devil's child.

My biological father was a plain-faced man of the cloth. A pervert. A hypocrite. A predatory beast. Finally, I have a name for him, and a backstory; knowledge to which I can attach all the hatred that was ever assigned to me. I can understand now why my mother despised me. I don't blame her. I was the by-product of a horrific ordeal that ruined her life, involuntarily playing a part in killing all chances of her creating a future with David Jones, the good-looking apprentice who'd given her a glimpse of hope after too many years of abject misery at Eden House. Eden House, the malignant place that had been rooted in my own history all along, more than I could have realised. Was that why Aunt Lyrica refused to talk to me about it? Or was it possible she didn't know the extent of what had happened to my mother, with the blessing of Sister Gregory, in that room adjoining the chapel?

I wonder if someone shamed my mother into keeping me. Or if she decided not to abort me or give me up, thinking perhaps she might learn to love me. It's a possibility, I suppose, but one that never transpired. I punctuated her life with shame, unhappiness and gross injustice. She should have given me away, done us both a favour.

As for Tom Dockin?

He was merely a figurative spectator at my conception. An idea sprouted from a seed of folkloric horror that had been planted and then grown over the years.

And yet.

And yet…

Did I truly believe that?

When I reached up and turned off the light, the darkness of the room was comforting. I no longer feared the shadows it kept.

I grinned; slight but audible. 'I am the Devil's child.'

The vampire's remains roused next to me. It took a pathetic breath into its collapsed lungs, its skin crawling on plush burgundy I could no longer see. Cockroaches and beetles danced on all surfaces, awakening the snakes that writhed inside the walls. On the bedside table, I could make out the ghostly outline of the plastic sachet I'd taken from Summer's room. It was empty.

I groaned; it was supposed to be a laugh. Did everyone seriously think I wouldn't look out for my little sister? I might be the Devil's child, but I'm not a monster. I wouldn't have let her take those drugs. Just as I wouldn't really have asked Tom Dockin to take her away. To eat her up. She's not Calanthe, after all. Besides, Tom Dockin's *my* monster. If my mother gave me anything at all, I realised now it was him.

Even though I accepted everything was ruined, and The Zoltan would never be my home, I felt at peace. Finally. I rested my head on my pillow and looked into the deepest shadows of the room, which were as black as a nun's habit. As deep as a vicar's sin.

'Tom Dockin, are you here?'

I didn't have to wait long till his huge form shuffled from the darkest corner, his smell emerging too, hot and heavy with the sebaceous oily secretions of an animal's skin collected in fur.

'What do you want Catherine Hall?' His voice was a low rasp and his tongue a scarred, blind thing that sought me in the dark.

'I'm not Catherine Hall,' I said. She was never me.

'Then who are you?'

The mattress beneath me moulded to my body like a welcoming womb. I sighed. 'I'm no one.'

'Everyone's someone, even me.'

'Make me believe it then.'

'Believe what you like.'

'I believe in you.'

'I know you do. But who are you?'

I closed my eyes. Imagined myself spinning in the ether behind the black space behind the moon which no one ever sees. Which no one knows exists. 'I'm the shadow of a shadow.'

'Whose shadow?'

'It doesn't matter.' I looked up and was shocked to find him standing over me. His defunct eyeballs were murky opals in the obscurity of his skull. His pallid skin translucent like a deep sea creature that's lived forever in the dark. 'Who are you?' I asked. 'Were you born into this world? Do you have a story? Were you once a man?'

'Once?'

'Ah. You think you still are? Yet you're so much more.' Like Dracula. This thought thrilled me. 'What happened to you, Tom Dockin? Who made you what you've become?'

I wasn't sure he'd answer. His silence was thick with shadows that morphed and taunted, prodding my skin. But then he said, 'The darkness.'

My heart sped up, his answer like an epiphany. 'You're the only one who ever fully accepted me. The only one who might do as I ask without boundary,' I said. 'So can you make all of this stop? Can you take me into the darkness?'

'Yes.' His metal teeth glinted, and he hunched closer. The smell of him so heady, I thought I might faint. 'I can do that.'

'Will it hurt?'

'Very much.' He lifted my hand and put my fingers into his mouth, his lips were chafed but moist and the serrated edge of his teeth punctured my skin where they touched.

'You are nearest and dearest and all the world to me,' I said, closing my eyes again, quoting Mina Harker. 'Our souls are knit into one, for all life and all time.'

He snorted a blast of goat-breath through his nose – in humoured acceptance or derision to my sentimental heart-pouring – then bit down, severing flesh, muscle and tendon, and crunching bone. White hot pain flashed up my arm. Stars danced behind my eyes. The vampire exploded into a million fireflies.

I have crossed oceans of time to find you.

I lay still and endured; that was all.

Epilogue

Dan Munro

Kendra answered on the fifth ring. She sounded annoyed. 'What do you want?'

'I, er, just wanted to say sorry. For everything.'

There was silence on the other end.

The bedside lamp flickered, and a shadow moved across the wall as though someone had walked in front of it. Dan rocked forward on the bed, looking for something that could have made the shape. A moth crossing the surface of the bulb, its silhouette a magnified shadow play, perhaps.

There was nothing.

He shivered, settling back against the headboard and pulling the duvet tighter to his bare chest. Now he thought about it, the room had a chill he'd not noticed before.

'Are you drunk?' Kendra asked. Which was a fair question.

'No.' Which was sort of the truth. 'I've been doing a lot of thinking these past couple of days, that's all, and I want to come home. I want to be with you and the kids.'

'Hmmm. How many times have I heard that?'

'I mean it. This time's different.' He could imagine Kendra rolling her eyes. 'I miss you all. Even the stupid dog.'

Kendra fell silent.

Was that a good sign? Was she realising how much she missed him and therefore contemplating that maybe she should give their marriage one more try? Because Dan was under no illusion, this would be his last chance.

'Can we meet up?' he asked when she still hadn't replied. Gentle coercion.

'When?'

'Tomorrow night? Or I can do the day after? Whenever's good for you.'

'Whenever's good for me?' Scorn laced her voice. 'Are you sure you can fit me in? Do you really have the time?'

Dan massaged his forehead and took a deep breath. 'Please, Kendra.'

She made an unhappy sound, then said, 'Okay. I'll meet you the day after tomorrow.'

'Great. Name the time and place. I'll be there.'

'Call me in the morning, at a respectable hour. We'll talk about it then.'

'Okay.'

'Night, Dan.' She hung up.

Dan's heart relaxed somewhat, and a joyous warmth spread outwards from the cosy cavity where it beat at the prospect of going home. He leaned across and turned off the bedside lamp. Needed to get some sleep. For the past few days, he'd been checking out the proposed site for an underground amusement park. Draculand. He was a project manager for Kraken Attractions and was overseeing this venture in North Yorkshire. He'd met with engineers and spoken to people from the Environment Agency, and there were no restrictions that might hamper the work. He could head back to Glasgow and do some prepping and planning from there – and spend some time with his family.

What about friends? the sadistic part of his conscious mind wanted to know. Will you make time for them too?

Dan clenched his fists so tightly his nails bit into his palms. Don't. Don't do this.

You should always make time for friends though,

shouldn't you? Especially those in need.

His stomach twisted with the usual dread this kind of inner monologue brought with it, giving him an instinctive craving for a large shot of whisky. He ground his teeth together, so hard his jaw hurt.

This has got to stop.

How can it ever?

Because it wasn't my fault.

Wasn't it?

No. And I can't keep blaming myself for what happened.

Can't you?

No.

Steve was your best friend.

How could I have known what would happen?

You should have, but you were the worst mate ever.

A noise by the wardrobe on the opposite wall drew Dan's attention, making his body react in a rash of gooseflesh. It was an odd metallic grating. Rhythmic, but unidentifiable. He supposed it might come from the room next door, but it sounded too close. He sat up and squinted into the dark corner, seeing only the usual cluster of shadows there. But then a sudden movement made him jump. A large hulking mass stepped forward, freeing itself from the wardrobe's obscurity. And what was that awful stink?

Heart beating wildly, Dan flung his arm out and flicked on the bedside lamp, expecting to find an intruder.

But there was nothing to see. No one there.

Still that smell though. An overwhelming feeling of dread too.

A perpetual cycle of destruction, he thought to think.

And still that sound.

Snip snip snip.

Acknowledgements

When embarking on the literary journey of writing this book, Bram Stoker's *Dracula* and Francis Ford Coppola's 1992 film *Bram Stoker's Dracula* massively inspired me. I first read *Dracula* when I was around fifteen or sixteen, after watching the film, and I remember it captured my imagination like no other book had. I love visiting Whitby, each time finding myself immersed in wistfully romantic *Dracula* vibes. And I knew one day I'd write a book that somehow incorporated both Whitby and *Dracula*, as a tribute to two of the things that have given me great pleasure over the years.

Straight away I decided I wanted to create a story that wasn't strictly vampire related, but would embrace the theme of *Dracula* nonetheless. I was keen to work with a different fiend altogether, so when I stumbled across some information online about an obscure folkloric figure called Tom Dockin, who has pointed iron teeth and a clear blood-lust, he seemed like the perfect antagonist for me to explore and adapt. I'd never heard of him before and was excited to give an ambiguous – possibly even forgotten about – bogeyman character from olden days some limelight in a modern setting.

The italicised sentences within *The Shadow of a Shadow* are quotes from *Dracula*. I purposefully stylised the book this way so they are easily identifiable. To ensure they are properly acknowledged, the passages I took from *Dracula* are:

'I have crossed oceans of time to find you.'
'I am longing to be with you, and by the sea, where we can talk together freely and build our castles in the air.'

'Perhaps at the end the little things may teach us most.'
'Doctor, you don't know what it is to doubt everything, even yourself.'
'Loneliness will sit over our roofs with brooding wings.'
'I am all in a sea of wonders. I doubt; I fear; I think strange things, which I dare not confess to my own soul.'
'You are nearest and dearest and all the world to me. Our souls are knit into one, for all life and all time.'
'I lay still and endured; that was all.'

I also took the line *'See me. See me now.'* from the scene in Coppola's *Bram Stoker's Dracula* (when Dracula is willing Mina to see him amongst the crowd) and used it when Catherine is willing Dracula to see her in the amusement arcade. It seemed perfect for the moment.

Thanks to Hannah Thompson for editing *The Shadow of a Shadow*, and for the sound advice that was offered. It's always massively appreciated!

Thanks to Delilah for always being by my side, even when I didn't have biscuits.

Thanks to Benn Clarkson for formatting the hardcover files. We'll go to the pub sometime, and I'll buy you a pint. Maybe? We can but hope the pubs will open again.

Thanks to family members and friends for being there when it mattered most.

Thanks to Kimberly Yerina and Karl Hartley for the continued support and encouragement on social media. It's massively appreciated by me, as an indie author, to have people who read so vastly within the horror genre championing my work. Much respect!

Thanks to Derek, without whom none of this would be possible. Your unending love, support and encouragement is everything!

And last, but not least, thanks to you, my reader, for allowing me to share my love of storytelling with you.

I think it's safe to say I'm not done with Tom Dockin or

Whitby yet. I can hear the *snip snip snip* of Tom Dockin's jagged teeth in my head as new ideas take shape in the shadows that have been cast by this book. Maybe next time we'll follow Dan Munro as he continues his project management of Draculand. Or perhaps we'll go right back to the very start and explore the roots of Tom Dockin himself. The man behind the bogeyman.

About The Author

R. H. Dixon is a horror enthusiast who, when not escaping into the fantastical realms of fiction, lives in the northeast of England with her husband and whippet.

Visit her website for horror features, short stories, promotions and news of her upcoming books: **www.rhdixon.com**

IF YOU ENJOYED READING THIS BOOK, PLEASE LEAVE A REVIEW ON AMAZON. THANK YOU!